CW00386400

The And

Christopher Hall

First published in 2018

Copyright © Christopher Hall 2018

Christopher Hall asserts the moral right to be identified as the author of this work

Cover design by Sarah Beaudin

ISBN 9781726704663

This novel is entirely a work of fiction. The names, characters and incidents portrayed in it are the work of the author's imagination. Any resemblance to actual persons, living or dead, events or localities is entirely co-incidental.

All rights reserved. No part of this publication may be reproduced, stored in a retrieval system, or transmitted, in any form or by any means, electronic, mechanical, photocopying, recording or otherwise without the prior permission of the author.

This book is sold subject to the condition that it shall not, by way of trade or otherwise, be lent, re-sold, hired out or otherwise circulated without the author's prior consent in any form of binding or cover other than that in which it is published and without a similar condition including this condition being imposed on the subsequent purchaser.

to Carol

1.

I have died several times in my lifetime, but this time it's different. If it's to be a public event then I intend to shape it. If the Internet is to be the courtroom then I have no choice but to become my own advocate. And if others are to be condemned with me then I don't know if I can stand idly by and watch. Like every chronicler before me, trying to keep up with the world as it moves beyond his capacity to capture it, I am using the past to explore the future; a future that I never imagined could happen. You might just be the last witness to it, the reader I can appeal to before it's all over for me. This is not intended to be the diary of a suicide. The death I refer to is not a literal death. This is an account of how I became a cybernetic man. The old me, the one I am leaving behind was different. He used to feel and think in a completely different way. Emotion came naturally without having to imitate or repeat an automated response. He was simple and idealistic in his appreciation of the sensual world. Above all, I don't recall that he was aware of something called his 'programming'. He would have laughed at people who denied that love exists. I don't know if there are any readers out there who still do believe in it. Do you? And so I'm nostalgic and regretful at the same time. I don't want the robot to replace the man without some testimony about how this happened. I can't bear the idea of the old self being replaced without the decency of a valediction, however simple. If it's just me that's writing, if it's just me typing for the sake of typing then at the very least I want to have something to point to and say 'Beware.' Isn't that why we're all typing now?

My name is Richard Kidd. I know, I know it's one of

those ridiculous names like P. Brain or R. Sole, but my parents didn't think of it that way. They named us all after kings and queens. My brother James and sister Liz might have got off fairly lightly but as a native Mancunian I never really minded the R Kidd. I like the bemused expressions of hotel staff when I check in or the slight pause that happens whenever I have to phone up a call centre and they clock my accent. I'm happy that my name makes people smile. It's effortless and what could be more satisfying than that? I worked as a creative director for a small independent ad firm in Old Street called The Witchetty Grub. Did you see the Pisco Sour ads? What about Atlantis tyres or the denim ads I did for the designer Fidel? Anyway, I got the push. It was my profession, my life, for about ten years. We were taken over by the media giant Wordfarm and they didn't take too kindly to failure. I'm thirty-five with the short, greying locks of someone of forty-something. I've lived in London ever since I moved south but not any more. I was engaged to be married to a girl I met at a launch party. Helen and I aren't together anymore. We lasted for five years. We might have been married now, we might have had a child together. It's a life that will never be realised.

So, what am I doing now? You could probably look it up on Facebook or Linkedin but what would that tell you? Would you trust it? Give a man a few words to say and a camera and he can lead you to a perfect mirage. Give him a free reign and more often than not he'll hang himself. I'm a struggling photographer living off my redundancy. You won't find that online. I'm bunkered down in an apartment by the sea where I moved to fulfil the dream of getting out of the agency world to become a real artist. This was the plan. It was our plan and then like a carefully planted roadside mine it all exploded around me until I became so dazed and shell-shocked that I could barely speak to anyone. When I started to come round, when I came back to reality, I realised that something was different. Something was different about my condition, a sudden and traumatic arrival like the start of a growth, a lipoma that you notice one day underneath your skin and can't help touching afterwards. If there is still time I'd like to reverse it. I'd like to stop it happening at all. You see, I am in the business of future prevention. Let me start with a breath of fresh air. It was only a few weeks ago.

I flung the sash window upwards and leant half-way out into the simmering air. The air. The beautiful sun. The sea. The coastline stretching to my left and right. A place of rest and a new life. The sky was a beautiful pale blue. One of my greatest pleasures on waking up is to cast my eyes on a beautiful blue sky. For me, it's best to view it from the window of an upper-floor bedroom. It's one of the first things I look for when I look around a house. I skirt around the other features and head straight towards the window. I love the colours of the sky, its sometimes intense stillness or the texture of the clouds passing underneath it. It has different expressions, like a god and although its condition can be measured by scientists and de-mystified by meteorologists it can still be yours. When you wake up and draw the curtains back, that particular view of the sky is yours and belongs to you. No-one else has quite the same picture within the frame of their window pane. No photograph could do it justice although God knows I've tried. If I could capture one feature of the sky on film, it would be the sense of distance that you get when you try to look through it to see what lies behind the blue curtain. It seems to go on forever and no matter how hard you try you can never feel that you have got to the end. It was the view I had been searching for.

'What do you think? Some people think it's a cliché, the ferris wheels, the crazy golf but not me. I love it,' said the girl behind me.

I turned around half-expecting her to be beaming at me

and twirling the house keys on her forefinger, but she had her arms crossed and looked like I was the tenth person she had felt obliged to say this to that day. It didn't seem to bother her that I didn't answer her question.

'Would you like to follow me to the second bedroom?'

She smiled and simply led me past the staircase and to the other side of the apartment where I could smell the slightly dizzying odour of bleach coming from the nearby bathroom. It was not hard to see a feminine presence. An oil burner and candles situated on one corner of the bath tub gave it away. The bedroom was large enough for my needs and could fit a small studio.

'Will you take it do you think?' asked the estate agent.

'I like it but…I'll need to check with my partner.'

Something in my reaction irritated her and I could detect a slight quiver in the corners of her mouth. I liked the flat. I wanted it, but I didn't want to jump the gun. 'People love these flats. Developers and landlords snap them up. I'd much prefer it to go to a nice couple who will give it the love it needs. If it was up to me…….well it's your decision.'

'OK, I've got a good feeling about the place. I'll take it,' I answered.

She beamed and lunged towards me to shake on the deal. I thought she might hug me for a moment.

'Shall we head back to the office for the paperwork?' she said.

I followed her out of the room and down the stairs, matching her step for step until we were outside the house and back on the street. If I had realised then what was about to unfold would I have done something to stop it? If I had known what a nightmare this flat would come to represent would I have been so hasty? I might have done myself a favour by trying to seduce her on the stairs. A slap in the face might at least have woken me up and given me an excuse.

I climbed into the cramped front passenger seat of her

little hatchback and we zoomed off to the office. On the journey back I tried calling Helen, but she wasn't picking up. I tried again a couple of minutes later and got her voicemail. I left a message, gabbling something about how great it all was and how we were finally going to break free. The estate agent, whose name was Matilda, beamed at me and ran through the gearbox like it was a toy as she braked and accelerated up and down side streets before we reached the seafront. I imagined that she must hear all kinds of childish excitement from Londoners gushing over a bit of commuter real estate. I put the phone back in my pocket.

'How long have you been working as an estate agent?'

'Only six months. I used to work in London, but we all got let go when the recession hit.'

'How do you find it?'

'It's ok. It gives me a chance to get out of the office. Do you mind if I smoke?' she asked when we had got stuck at the lights. She beamed at me keenly again. As the lights changed, she was still trying to find her lighter.

'Here,' I said holding her handbag still as she fumbled around inside. The blare of a horn made her jump and she glanced briefly at the green light in front of us and pulled out a packet of cigarettes. Several more horns hooted behind us.

'And the same to you!' yelled Matilda holding up a finger to the rear view mirror and taking her first puff. With a couple of ragged and nervous gear changes we were off, seconds before the lights turned red again.

'Sorry,' she said, 'it's been a stressful day.'

'Don't worry. We all have them,' I said and I glanced at her feet as they moved between the clutch and the accelerator. The split in her skirt had fallen open exposing the thigh of her right leg. I tried staring out of the window.

'What are you going to do with the flat when you move in?' asked Matilda.

'I'm setting up a photographer's studio.'

'Is that what you do for a living?'

'No but I'm about to.'

'I love photography,' said Matilda smiling at me, 'I did my MA in Modern Art.'

I nodded. In my profession everyone I meet claims to like art, goes to exhibitions, takes photographs, knows how to play an instrument and is working on a new screenplay.

'I got asked to pose nude for an artist last year. He just came up to me in the street and asked me. Can you believe that?'

'Believe it or not I can believe it. Did you?'

'Well, yes I did in the end when I'd checked him out online.'

Matilda laughed to herself and went slightly red. I wondered if she had said this just because it had popped into her head. She finished her cigarette and tossed it out of the window and then adjusted her skirt to cover her legs. I tried Helen again. This time the phone was engaged. When we arrived back at the estate agents, I followed Matilda to her desk. 'Can I get you a tea or a coffee while we wait for her to get back to you?' she asked. I asked for tea and she disappeared into a room in the back office for a few minutes. Two other estate agents, both young men, were noisily tapping at keyboards. One of them, a tall and chunky looking blonde, nodded in my direction and smiled.

'How are you sir? Did you find everything as you wanted?' he asked.

He stuck a tongue in his lower lip as if he had some kind of object trapped in his mouth. Before I could answer I felt my phone start to go off, vibrating and growling in my jacket pocket. It was Helen.

'What is it Richard? I'm busy.'

'Didn't you get my message?' I said quietly.

'What? Yes.'

'So what do you think?'

'Rich. We need to talk about things.'

10

Matilda had returned with two mugs of tea and was smiling at me hopefully.

'What's wrong?' I asked.

I watched the smile on Matilda's face begin to fall and with one finger raised indicated that I needed to step out of the office.

'It's not that,' said Helen, 'we need to talk about things.' This wasn't the answer I expected. Only the day before she had given me the reigns over the whole issue of moving. Now she wanted a debate.

'Sorry, I don't understand. We agreed this a while ago. What do we need to talk about?'

'Just things,' she went on, 'Everything.'

'Such as? I mean can you be more specific?'

'Rich it's everything. Us. You. Me. Everything. Look, I can't talk about this now.' She hung up.

I dialled her number and waited for her to pick up. There was no answer.

I walked back into the office and asked Matilda for a pen so that I could sign the contracts. I knew full well that I was taking it and that nothing, not even a momentary wobble from Helen, would change my mind. So I signed and marched back to my car, pushing it to the limit to get back up the motorway to London.

By the time I hit the outskirts of the city I had begun to feel tired. We'd been living for the last few years in a two bedroom in Swiss Cottage. It was a nice place, but we spent very little of our waking lives occupying it except as a refuge from our work. At weekends we would come together and build our lives around making it our place. For years this had been good for both of us but I had started to get anxious as to where it was all leading. I turned into the drive in front of the building and switched off the engine, looking up at a picture of a life made up of love, interesting work, friendships, cultural variety; all the things I imagined that I once wanted. I don't know how long I waited in the car before going in. I remember that it started to get dark. I turned the lights on all over the flat from the lounge to the kitchen and looked in the cupboards for something to eat. Nothing appealed to me. I opened a bottle of wine and stretched out on the sofa in front of the TV, to play Helen's waiting game, becoming more convinced with each sip that Helen would arrive, tired, overworked perhaps, but ready to share whatever had been troubling her over a drink.

It was the shrill ring-tone of the phone that woke me up. I'd drifted off to sleep and had no idea how much time had passed or how long I'd been asleep. I knocked over my glass and stumbled to the phone before the voicemail kicked in. It was Helen.

'Where are you?' I said, 'I've been waiting ages for you. What time is it?'

'It's late. I'm at mum and dads. I think I'm going to stay here for the night.'

'I'll come over and pick you up.'

'No. You sound like you've been drinking.'

'What do you mean?'

'Rich. It sounds like you've already made up your mind to move out. I might ask you when you're going?'

'Helen, can you tell me what's happening? I thought we were both moving. You're being irrational about this. I can cancel the contract. I just thought we'd better not let it go.'

There was silence.

'I'm really sorry about this Rich. I know you're going to hate me. I never thought it would be like this,' Helen's voice trembled. Then I heard her say the words, 'I'm leaving.'

I sank to the floor, knocking my head against the bookshelf behind me.

'I don't understand.'

I listened for a response, not wanting to continue with the conversation but not able to tear myself away from full impact, like an unwitting witness to a car accident. Everything seemed to crowd my attention all at once as if the whole gaze of the world was upon me or like an actor on the stage in the spotlight, blocking out any awareness of anything but his own breathing and the pauses in between. The sound of Helen's tears, the muffled voice of her mother in the background, the creaking floor beneath me all crowded into my eardrums.

'Are you sure? Are you serious?'

'Of course I'm serious,' she sobbed.

'I never saw this. Where did this come from?'

'I've not been happy for years.'

'What do you mean years? How long? I mean when did you say anything?'

'I couldn't ok. I just couldn't.'

'Then why? Are you seeing someone else?'

'I can't talk to you now. I'm too tired to talk to you about this now. I'm so so sorry.'

The words made sense. My mind flooded with rivers of converging memories and feelings. There had been her anxiety about contraceptives, evenings out with friends that she would never talk about and time, an endless stream of time, stolen from our relationship by the digital screen of our laptops. As these moments and images sprang to the very forefront of my mind I had the odd feeling that this is exactly what I had been expecting her to say and, at the same time, a numbing stab of shock and disbelief. It was as if I had floated outside my body and could see myself, immobilized and stupefied, but nevertheless able to recognize that this is where my relationship would eventually end; in disaster or disgust, betrayal or resentment, escapism or violence and it seemed perfectly reasonable to me that there was nothing and nowhere in between these extremes.

'I'm sorry,' sobbed Helen at the other end of the line.

There was nothing I could think of to say.

I hung up. It was too shocking for me to think about and too much pain to take in. I knelt down on the floor and began to hit it solidly with my fists. Looking back, I feel ashamed to admit this, but every punch was aimed at an imagined rival, the enemy who had taken my life away from me. I backed into a corner and sobbed to myself 'No! No! No! No!' Need I go on? I think I wandered around the flat, pacing between rooms like a madman. Tiredness eventually crept up on me like a velvet glove, stroking my eyes shut and lifting my frame upstairs into bed where I curled up and fell asleep. Perhaps some people might have expected me to run out into the street and scream or yell abuse at Helen down the phone. They might have expected me to sob and smash dishes or burn photographs. I know that's how people expect a rejected man to behave. Of course some men do turn into a Bad Wolf, burning the whole house down and killing everyone inside. Have you read the papers recently? There seems to be a new one every other week. The truth is I stopped feeling. That's how it was. Emotion seemed to fall away from me that night and all I could think about was how to achieve my own personal oblivion and erase all those horrible sentimental memories of a past that now began to take on a fake and sinister hue.

2.

I woke up the next day with bruised hands and a sore throat. I tried to go back to sleep and each time I closed my eyes the crushing news of the night before muscled its way into the forefront of my mind like a crusty old binge-drinker, staggering around and knocking everything out of his way. Why do our minds seek resolution before we understand the problem? What prompts us to seek the conclusion of things that are in the process of following their own trajectory? Is it that we still believe that if we were to think of an idea, act in a new way, plan a new strategy the trajectory of the event could still be worked successfully in our favour? Or is to stop the pain at any cost? Perhaps it's not like this for everyone but I can be sure that my mind will never leave me alone until it senses that the end of uncertainty is near. Food, drink, work nor any activity I can think of will drive it away.

It was Sunday. Helen used to recover from her hangovers on a Sunday. I lay in bed and tried not to think at all. My memory of what happened next is like a dream; blurred with lots of drifting from one thing, from one place to another. I remember that I gave up trying to sleep and got out of bed and walked to the park. I think I phoned Helen again. Well, I'm pretty sure I did but there was no answer. I wandered around. The other lonely souls walking their dogs and sauntering around with their bags of stale bread for the ducks filled me with dread and all I could do was to go back, mentally, and plunge myself feet first into the past.

We had been together for five years. We first met each other at university in Manchester. I always assumed that I fell in love with her first. I was always falling in love at that age with little if any regard for the varieties of love on offer. So many of the women in the city's pubs or at the lecture hall or the student party must have crossed my path, but I ignored all of them in favour of Helen, waiting for the day when I fully expected her relationship with her boyfriend to collapse. It never happened. I fell in love with Helen quickly and brutally and then lost contact with her for a while until our paths crossed again by chance some eight or nine years later. She walked into a product launch in London for one of my clients and looked immaculate and dazzling in a dark trouser suit and red necktie. As soon as I spotted her sipping from a glass of bubbly and delicately stroking the arms of the people around her, I realised she was still the same girl; tactile, affectionate, generous, spirited. (Also, very intractable, stubborn and secretive). She recognized me immediately and moved in my direction leaving behind her tribe of followers. I remember her turning an observation about my prematurely greying hair into a compliment. I can picture her squeezing a business card into my hand and ordering me to keep in touch. I did, after trying to talk myself out of it and gratifyingly discovered that she was single. Just over a year later and she was arriving at my doorstep with a removal van, carting her things into my flat and then running around trying to help me pick the right sofa or that extra special antique for the lounge. To outsiders and especially to her friends it often looked as though she was more devoted to me than the other way around.

We were in love. At least, I believed we were. It's funny how these things can't easily be verified with the passage of time. Memories should confirm the truth of an emotion but as I try to go back the further the memory recedes into the distance the less confidence I have. Now that the relationship is over the ties that bound me to her have loosened and with them my moorings. The frustration I feel now is that I can only see the facts of what we did; the reunion meeting at the launch party, the first date in Soho, the holiday in Xanthi, the proposal in New York. They are more like snippets of a film in which I was playing a role for a while. I think I was happy. I seem to remember being in love. I recall events but the feelings? No. There is absolutely no certain emotion that I can bring back to life and verify that it ever existed. Even birthday cards, little notes, anniversary cards only demonstrate that an emotion was expressed but not that the emotion was true or even the simulation of something that felt true. All I can really say is that I think we were in love. It didn't occur to me then that this was the first glimmer of a new state of being, but the transition from pure feeling to a distant photographic view of life was starting to emerge.

I called on a friend of mine from the agency world. His name is Anders Svedberg. This is a man who has remained as constant in my life as Helen. He's a Swede. He's honest and straightforward and that's always appealed to me. We worked together on a number of ads for a brand of elite Swiss watches high up in the French Alps and immediately hit it off. He enjoys a life of seemingly professional bliss and personal freedom as an independent consultant on web marketing. Not for him the rush of the agency life anymore but he says he likes it. He's never married, and I've lost track of the number of times he changes his girlfriends. As always he sounded as though he had only just woken up, 'Oh. Er. Hello Rich. Yeah. How are things?' he said as he answered the phone. 'Come on over.'

When I arrived at his flat his reaction was not what I had been expecting.

'Surprised? No Richard. I'm sorry but I'm not surprised,' he said, 'It's not possible to be surprised by something that happens all the time. Some of my girlfriends had affairs with me before they decided to leave their boyfriends. I'm sorry it happened to you of course. It's a big problem but you couldn't have done anything to change it.'

'I'm shocked,' I said.

'Yes. That is perfectly natural,' said Anders, 'Shocked is what we feel when we encounter something we didn't expect to happen.'

'What am I going to do Anders? How can I go on?'

'You can do many things of course. If you would like my opinion, then I would suggest that you do nothing.'

'Nothing? I need to get to the bottom of this.'

'Well, you can of course. Then you will have to ask yourself the question why. Why did she do this? Why did he do it? Why did it happen to you? The only answer you can get to these questions is bad ones, never good. It's always something bad about you or life itself. Would you let me to give you the benefit of some advice?'

I was too stunned to resist.

'Let Helen deal with the problem,' he said, 'Send her a message to say that you are going to move out. Don't get crazy, keep in touch every few weeks and soon she will come round. Go on a trip or go to this place you have by the sea. Take photographs and continue with your life. Then when you have taken time, you'll know what's good for you. I think she will come back. The appeal of the new guy will wear off.'

The new guy. I can't stop until I know exactly who and when and all that. It's driving me crazy,' I said.

'I know.'

Anders tried to change the subject and began to show me the prototype for an app he had been developing for a client. He talked about as if it were an entity. Anders' client was trying to establish a website with one view of a customer's finances that would always find the best economies for their money. It wasn't long before his sonorous voice sent me drifting off.

'I'd better go,' I said, 'Thanks.'

I remember his parting words, 'Don't go crazy Rich.

Remember that. I'll help you move when you're ready. You know, I might even move down there with you.'

As I left Anders's flat it occurred to me that I ought to envy him. What he had lost in not finding a woman he wanted to stay with, he had more than made up for in the relationships he had accumulated over the years. The Colombian painter, the Italian teacher, the Norwegian student all blended perfectly into a litany of saintly and sometimes not so saintly women. This man; who had never had a relationship that had lasted more than two years, who had never had a child, who had never married or divorced; how could he give advice about the heart? What right did he have to tell me what I should do? Well that's the trick. Anders never gave advice from the heart. I remember thinking, 'What if he's right? What if the only answers we get to the question 'Why?' are bad ones?'

I got back to my flat which had taken on the atmosphere of an empty hotel room. It seemed larger somehow and colder. The photographs on the wall depicting Helen and I together, were like forgotten billboard advertisements, where the peeling sheets reveal the traces of another poster underneath that once promised a new and exciting brand from a company that has since gone bust. I made myself a drink and switched on my laptop, briefly checking my Browsing History. It's a noble pursuit isn't it, browsing history? Forget Gibbon, Macaulay and Hobsbawm. Browsing history used to help us to uncover a sense of the continuity of the past with the present. It helped us to understand who we are and where we've come from. Now it means something entirely different. Its electronic fingerprint of where we've been is a repository of guilt and something to guard against discovery. It is a record of the chaotic psychosis of everyday life. Yet it's also a map of how pre-determined and routine our thought processes can be. It's a catalogue of what we think about. Browsing History is real time history and it's both dispensable and retrievable at the same time. Is it merely a history of connections between concepts brought to life by the conscious mind? Or is it more subliminal than that, like word association or automatic writing, driven by the invasive social engineering of my own profession? Have you looked at your own browsing history recently? I wonder if it says more about what you desire than you would care to think.

Without access to Helen's computer I had no hope of getting hold of her browsing history and that more than anything was what I was curious to uncover. She had taken her laptop with her. When I look back at our life together Helen never closed the door to the study but would sit opposite the entrance with the lid of her laptop raised like a protective drawbridge. It didn't bother me at the time. I was often sitting across from her looking at my own laptop. Now, I began to wonder what she had been looking at especially in the evenings when I had grown tired and gone to bed. It had been rare for me to outlast her in those stakes and she could keep going with instant messages and social media well into the early hours of the morning. Sometimes I would drift off to sleep to the tap, tap, tapping sound of her keyboard.

I looked around the flat. Helen had been back. I checked all the rooms and checked the wardrobes as if there might be an intruder in the house. She had taken most of her everyday clothes. Drawers had been left half-closed. The hairdryer, her spiky hair- brush and the straighteners that normally lay beside her side of the bed had gone. I went back to our little studio and switched on my laptop. It lay on the table like a clam. There were no new emails or messages. News travels fast but there was no evidence that anything was wrong in the online world. I checked Helen's social networks, her news feeds and status updates for anything that might hint at a smoking gun. There was not so much as a sympathetic hug, a poke or an emoticon to speak of from the last twenty-four hours. Unusually for her she had made no comments for several days. So I began to trawl her profile, looking back over the last six months in search of a change in mood or character. She had shared a lot about herself. I hadn't realised just how often she updated the world with her feelings;

Feeling like I'm drowning today.
Needs a glass of wine!
Not happy!
Needs a hug.
Great news! Can't believe it!
Someone is sending me good things today.

All of them elicited what I assumed were the desired responses. Even I was surprised to find how often I had replied and commented on these pieces of bait. Around the time I went off to film the Pisco adverts in Peru I had stopped commenting. There were other male commentators too, none of whom hinted at anything more sinister than a rather unctuous fascination with the absurd and the banal. She was a steady follower of her clients. I recognized them as the usual suspects, banks, mining companies, FTSE hangers-on, that she had been working with over the years. She followed fan sites of her favourite TV shows and novelists as well as the alma mater of her university and a reunion group she'd joined. The pictures uploaded from her mobile phone were a mix of PR parties, client launches, holidays we'd taken together. There was even a photo of us both hiking in Switzerland which I'd completely forgotten about.

None of this answered my main purpose. Why? Why had she ended it now? I wondered if she might also have been trawling through my life story to offer something up to her conscience. Did she find something that exonerated her? I had nothing to hide apart from…did I say that I'm not an innocent victim? There. I've said it. At least I'm honest. How many victims are these days? There was an indiscreet snog at a Witchetty Grub party but there was nothing online about that. Or the time I invited Natalie out for dinner and cocktails and thought about having an affair without really having one. I looked up all the social networking sites I knew about. She has hundreds and hundreds of friends. She is connected to everyone she has ever met it seems. Still I couldn't find anything. There were messages of love and support a plenty. She'd left lots of 'xxxx's and affectionate greetings to her friends, all of whom seemed to have new jobs, new boyfriends, new lives. You name it, there was something to get excited about on a daily basis. Then there were the photos. I thought I knew about her photos. I appeared in many of them after all, but I'd never bothered to browse the photos of her workmates or her friends. Helen is a very tactile person. She gives out affection to everyone and she gets it in gushes in return. There were pictures of men dancing with her, men siding up to her and putting their arms around her shoulders, there were group shots of men and women snuggling up to her. There were shots of her cheek to cheek with other women. Absurd as it might have been, I went over the pictures again and again to see if there was someone who looked like they might be the one. Was the guy in the grey V-neck with the spiky blonde highlights acting in jest or was he planting a camp kiss on her cheek with intent? Hopelessly I hovered over his image with the cursor. The name Andy Farrier popped up on the screen. She'd never mentioned him. Did she even know him? There were some new pictures that had only recently been added. Helen had been tagged in them only a few weeks ago. They were school photographs taken in the 1990's, all spiky hair and baggy jumpers. Someone called Josh Bates had posted them and tagged a number of the lads and girls from the same year. I'd forgotten how awkward Helen looked in her teens. Her tinted glasses, to help with her dyslexia, were too big for her face but she had a winning smile even back then.

I was interrupted by a call. It was Anders.

'What are you doing Rich?' he asked.

'Checking up on me?' I said.

'Yes.'

'I'm OK. Honestly. Don't worry about me.'

'Found anything?' Anders went on.

'No, I can't find a thing. It's impossible. She hasn't left a trace.'

'No unusual tags in photographs?'

'Some but I don't know who they are.'

'No unusual connections?'

'She has so many. Hundreds.'

'Don't waste any more of your time Rich. You have a life to live. Try to think of something else to take your mind off it. Go into work tomorrow.'

My money was on Josh Bates.

3.

So that's what I did and for a few days everything continued as if nothing had happened. It can only have been a week or so later that I slugged my way into the office to be greeted with the words, 'Rich, Tom said wants to see you straight away.'

It was Gilly, the Witchetty Grub receptionist and all-round go-getter and graduate intern. As a native of the Internet age, born in the early 90's she's probably more qualified than anyone else in the agency to comment on digital behaviour. Yet, like all of us she starts at the bottom.

'Did you have a heavy night?' she asked.

By then I think she knew me well enough to know the answer to that question, but she was polite about it. I suspect that she was less than impressed by the bacon roll that I was busy stuffing into my mouth. She belongs to a generation who abhor eating bread or bacon for that matter.

'You better smarten up Rich. Wordfarm have been in.'

She came out from behind her desk to straighten my jacket collar.

'Since when?'

'Since before everyone got here. They were already in Tom's office when I got here.'

'Tom doesn't get out of bed before nine!'

'Well they must have called him. I don't know.'

'Suits. Well, I'm not going to skip breakfast for anyone.'

As I made my way into the lift and pressed for the second floor it crossed my mind that this might be something unusual. Wordfarm rarely paid us a visit. Unless we hopped over to their place in Holborn to pay homage at their annual ra-ra, party-cum-conference our paths rarely crossed. Since the takeover of Witchetty they had kept our small creative team together to carry on pretty much as we had always done with one difference. Budgeting and ROI became the order of the day. Tom had always taken care of that. You see we had the awards, the glory, the most talked about ads of the last ten years. Bringing them in would be like inviting a swarm of wasps to a tea party. We got our inspiration straight out of the pyrotechnic, photogenic school of situationist copywriting. Strap yourself to the mast and head into the storm. We lived the life that only advertising used to make possible. If we wanted to go to the Sahara to race quad-bikes or swim with sharks off the coast of South Africa, we just did it. If it made good copy, we didn't think twice. We didn't really need Wordfarm or their money. They needed us to revive their flagging creative juices. As the doors to the lift opened, I recognised Natalie, my creative partner, art director, muse, the confidant that every creative director needs tapping at her keyboard. She spotted me as soon as I walked in and pointed to Skinner's office. In fact, Skinner doesn't really have an office. The gentle giant sits in with everybody else but on those occasions when he needs a bolt hole we have a number of glass goldfish bowls suitable for the purpose. I could see him leaning backwards, wearing his best corduroy jacket. There were a couple of men in there with him, dressed in black suits with their balding heads and backs to the glass partition.

'What's happening?' I said as Natalie beckoned to me.

'They're not happy with something,' she said

'Why?'

'All I know is that we got a very strange email from Wordfarm last night about putting the rest of the schedule on hold. I think Tom's seen you.'

I turned around to see Tom looking at me with his wrinkled eyes, smiling like a little boy who knows he's been caught doing something he shouldn't. The two suits turned around in their seats. I can't remember if they even had facial expressions but let's assume that they did and that they betrayed nothing.

Tom had shifted his considerable bulk out of his seat to open the glass door for me, but I pushed my way into the room before he could get there. The men in suits got up as if to shake hands but perhaps because of my abrupt entry or because of a professional lassitude they had cultivated for these types of occasion they just shuffled towards the exit.

'I appreciate this Tom,' said one, 'See you on Friday.'

With that they walked out of the goldfish bowl and back to their empire.

'Rich,' said Tom smiling, 'Why don't you sit down for a second?'

'What did they want?'

'That my friend was the account director for Dalahar Alex Trent and one of Wordfarm's PR gurus Justin Wishart. They were sent here on a mission, sent by the one and only Giles Freeman himself. I'm afraid there have been some complaints.'

'So? We tell them to get stuffed like we normally do.'

'Dalahar are not too happy with the way the Pisco ads have been handled.'

'It's early days. Give it time,' I said, 'They clocked up plenty of units in the first weekend. I had every bar from Soho to Shoreditch covered. They were out of drinks after only three hours.'

'I don't doubt that people have tasted the drink Rich, but things have taken a dive since then. Questions have been asked of the budget and what happened in Peru.'

'Well you know what happened. We went over this. The altitude sickness on the Andes for one. We couldn't let Leah fall over a cliff. We had to get medical back up. She's only ever posed in front of a mountain. Never on one. This was a different kettle of fish for her. You know how skinny she is.'

'I know. And completely off her head. Did you have anything to do with this?' asked Tom and he unfolded a tabloid newspaper from his lap, laying it on the table in front of me like an exhibit. The cover showed a picture of Leah Knight being carried out of a club, all doe eyes and fixed smile. The headline read - 'PISC -ED AS A FISH - Leah off head on coke during mountain ad.'

'Nice one. Very funny. What's the problem? She's like that,' I said, 'So, Leah uses it recreationally. She'd picked up some in a nightclub in Cuzco. It was a tiny amount. Hardly a drugs orgy. But it worked. I'm telling you she was like a new woman and the shoot was perfect. So pure and clear. You've seen the ads.'

'I've seen the ads and she looks beautiful. Look, I don't disapprove but that's not going to wash with Wordfarm. The Peruvian government have gone as far as making a complaint. They're fed up of tourists trying to make a buck by smuggling drugs out of the country. It doesn't look good.'

'What are they worried about? No, seriously. Think about it. It's pure gold. A product placement in a celebrity scandal story. You couldn't plan stuff like this.'

Tom looked down at his chubby stomach where he'd rested his crab-like hands.

'I'm sorry Rich,' he said, 'Let me come to the point. It's not the only thing they've complained about. I'm not sure how this story came out, but Dalahar's Chief Exec is due to appear before the parliamentary select committee on the role of advertising in binge drinking. They could go down the same route as cigarette advertising and ban the whole thing. They've got more moral crusaders on the committee than the X-Men combined. Need I say more? The drinks industry is terrified. Dalahar are getting scared-off by the negative fallout….. it could be catastrophic.'

'Is that all?'

'Well, no if you want to know the whole truth. They had

concerns over the budget, the hotels, the security bills, the whole cost of taking Leah Knight. Then the Chileans have complained that Pisco is their national drink and the bloody Peruvians are not happy that it doesn't specify who invented it.'

'So? We ride it out. The whole Chile-Peru rivalry was left ambiguous. The Andes that feature in the ads run through both territories.'

'Apparently it's not what Dalahar wanted. I'm sorry…. It couldn't have happened at a worse time….. The board have made some demands about bringing the group into line. And Dalahar say they want out. They'll take their drinks elsewhere unless Wordfarm take more control over creative direction. I don't know how to tell you any other way, but they insist that you step aside and leave.'

'What? Are they sacking me? Are you agreeing to this? You're not serious? But you are serious? But this isn't my fault. This is crazy. This is a witch hunt. I'm being nailed to a cross.'

I'd like to think that I can put a more coherent argument together in moments of crisis but in all honesty, I lost it. I can see how hard it must have been for Tom and no doubt he'd tried everything he could, but I have never been great at seeing the other point of view.

'It's not as if I have a choice,' Tom went on. 'I don't want to lose you. I've fought this for the last two hours. Believe me I've done everything I can. I've called Giles Freeman to see what I can do but…he's not taking any calls.'

I forget what he said after this. My memory remains a little vague on the subject as you might imagine. I recall him apologising and looking uneasily at the people outside the goldfish bowl who I didn't doubt were looking in. I didn't want to look at anyone. My life seemed to dance before my eyes and I saw, for a while, all that we had seen and done together condensed into a rapidly unravelling collection of far happier times.

Tom took me on when I was just twenty-three. He had been like an uncle; good-humoured, encouraging, giving me a licence to experiment. There had never been any consequences of failure with Tom because he had always been willing to tell the client they didn't know what they were talking about and pick up the tab. More often than not he proved that his judgement was right and the client's was wrong. When I did manage to summon the courage to look through the glass partition I could see everyone looking towards us. Tom had stopped speaking. I just didn't know what to say. I half expected to wake up.

'So what's going to happen to me?'

'I'll make sure you're OK. Don't worry. I can give you a good package to set you up for at least a year. It's the least I can do after all you've done for me. Take a sabbatical. Treat it as time off to recharge your batteries. Then when the dust has settled….you know I'd have you back like a shot. And if you want to jump straight back into work I can recommend you to some people.'

'I think I need a break Tom.'

'Ok.'

'Do you mind if I just sit here for a minute.'

We remained still for a while and I remember considering whether there was any way I could still get out of this without having to face the others outside.

'You know, I knew they hadn't come to congratulate me. Something about this campaign has been wrong from the start. It didn't feel right from the minute we took off for Lima. How on earth did the press pick up on this story anyway? I mean someone must have tipped them off. '

'I don't know Rich. Rumours circulate. Paparazzi are everywhere. Don't be hard on yourself. It will blow over. You'll be back. I'm probably next on their hit list.'

'Can I go now?' I said before leaving the building. The thing I regret the most is not giving him or anyone else in the building a kiss or a hug goodbye. I wanted to be buried alive or at the very least for the building to save me the trouble by collapsing inwardly on top of us. Sadly, it wasn't to be and I fled from the office without daring to look at anyone, not even Natalie.

When I got home I logged on to see if Helen had added anything online. There had been an update. It read quite simply, 'Helen Morris is no longer in a relationship.' That was it. It had become an undeniable fact. Quite a few people had 'liked' the announcement which was disappointing including one new couple who we'd only had over for a drinks party a few weeks ago. I think I'd had a few too many and said something derogatory about the company she worked for. Her closest friend, Angela had also given it a thumbs-up. No-one had written anything in response, but it felt like an ambush. I picked up my phone and dialled her number. It was engaged. I opened my email. Her change in status had also been sent to me directly. It's a very useful tool social media. I began to compose an email to Helen and was struggling to write anything that didn't quickly descend into a rant when a message appeared from Anders.

'Read me before you do ANYTHING,' was the title. I opened it up and it went like this, 'Just heard the news. So sorry. Don't fight it. Don't retaliate. Use it to change your life. A.S.'

There were two hyperlinks in the email.

I clicked on the first one. It was a link to a story; *10 legendary ad campaigns that flopped before becoming cult classics*, a humorous take on the worst faux pas, misplaced and misanthropic advertisements of all time. It was some consolation I suppose that whatever happened to Pisco would never be as bad at the advert for Heinz Soup which began 'Nowadays most husbands no longer beat their wives.' The second link was something completely different. What opened up on my screen was written by a psychologist at the University of Illinois and it dealt with the pathology of rejection. I could see what he was doing here but Anders being Anders would have wanted to get straight to the point. I scrolled through a few lines and began to read it. In amongst the text I found a sentence, highlighted by dozens of readers including Anders. It read;

"The effects of betrayal have a profound and disturbing effect upon the human psyche. Of these effects a neurophysiological study identified key hormonal alterations affecting the brain itself and subsequent social behaviour. Many of these changes have been found to be life-altering."

Hormonal alterations? Life-altering? Well, of course any kind of change can be described as 'life-altering' but filching it from an academic journal to prove a point was stretching it. I highlighted the text for future reference when I might be able to confirm or deny the precise degree to which my life had been altered. Flicking back over the pages again I find the study less than revelatory. The more people felt rejected or betrayed the less they trusted others around them. A drop in levels of the hormone oxytocin was identified as the main agent in all of this. The hormone acted as a sort of transmitter of love and contentment. I read on, discovering later on that social relationships had been improved when the hormone was added using a nasal spray. It seemed improbable but was taken very seriously by the academics in the field who had presumably tried it. I skip back now to re-read those life-altering effects on the human psyche that had so captivated me in that first paragraph. The list was by no means exhaustive but included "damage to the cognitive function in the brain", "a reduced ability to learn", "social isolation leading to suicidal thoughts", "a tendency to alter memories", "social phobias" and "a decreased sense of self". Perhaps a tendency to over-think problems could have been thrown in there for good measure. Still, the article didn't give any clues as to exactly how many of these consequences could be directly combated with a nasal spray. I've checked Amazon and they are asking people to stump up $59.99 for a tiny vial of oxytocin. Customer reviews were mixed but one woman claimed that it had given rise to her husband cleaning the house. If they could slip it into the water supply the world might change. It's the very essence of consumer aspiration. The boy who gets knocked back by a girl can take a spray to get him back out into the world again. Who wouldn't want to remedy a missing part of their brain in much the same vein as dying grey hair or getting your cracked teeth repaired?

I guessed that Anders had sent these links as a kindness. What can you trust in a world where everything and everyone's digital identity is a promotional advertisement for themselves? But not Anders. I could see some truth in the thesis. Something was missing inside me and I would need something stronger than a nasal spray to plug the void. I realised I was not alone. The vast, carnival of human experience that can be glimpsed through an online lens in all its diversity and extremity picked me up.

In Anders' email I recognized the Internet as guardian, that inner witness of the strangeness of one's self, reflecting the thoughts of millions in a coherent whole that makes madness commonplace and strangeness normal. I read on late into the night until I noticed the clock in the bottom corner of my laptop, several hours had passed and it was getting on for the early hours of the morning. This alternative mind had sucked away some of the pain of being in a singular time and place and as I headed for the bedroom I could still hear the cheerful echo of the laptop updating itself as I took off my clothes and folded back the duvet.

4.

So there we have it. This chronicle of mine is partly up to date but never quite of the moment. As I write this several more weeks have passed by. I had toyed with the idea of filming a live daily or weekly diary, but this leaves no room for editorial licence. And I'm not sure I like the idea of my grumpy face peering back at me in ten years' time like a wandering spirit haunting himself as the ghost of Internet Past. So a slightly irregular update like this is probably the best way to catalogue my various sins and errors. If you've ever read any of the great chroniclers of the past (Froissart? Bede? C.S.Lewis?) you'll know that a chronicle is not really what it seems. Despite the appearance of being a report from the past it's more about coming to terms with something in the present. It could be a war, a revolution, an expedition or something as simple as an illness. In my case it's an evolving piece about the successive shocks that my flesh is heir to. I have moved out and as I sit here surrounded by the stare of a solitary light-bulb in the darkened windows of my new home I feel as though I should bring you up to date.

So what's it been like? I realised that no amount of clinging on to our old home was going to help and as I'd already signed up to the new flat I decided to go ahead with it. Unless Helen was willing to meet and talk there seemed little point in tormenting myself further by delaying the inevitable. Anders said I had to get on with it, to move on and find a new way of living. Tom has been true to his word and sent a generous redundancy package to my account. I don't need to work now for at least a year. A tumultuous farewell party from everyone at the Witchetty Grub had embroiled me in a three day bender and a hangover that steadfastly refused to shift. Looking at my face in the mirror I can see that skipping the usual daily rituals of razor and shower have changed me. For the better I might add. I brought a few possessions with me; the art books that I've carried around since university and some of my sketches, drawings and photographs. There's a black bin-liner full of shoes and hats and belts and stuff, a couple of suits hanging behind the bedroom door and a suitcase full of clothes that I've only half unpacked. The temporary wardrobe I've erected is tiny and I'll need to buy another one but there's no rush. Lastly, there's the camera equipment and the Nikon, a thirtieth birthday present from Helen. Gathering my belongings together has been a rushed job. I didn't leave a note or a letter, didn't say goodbye to any of our neighbours. I didn't stop to look back as I dragged the cases and bags into the car. It was raining and all I wanted to do was get the car filled up as quickly as possible before heading off. It wasn't long before I was on my way and pulled out of the small car park located behind our block of flats and joined the flow of traffic heading towards the M25.

Now this car is my property, but Helen and I used to share it. I paid for it and we jointly owned it. She's got a set of keys. The way I see it is that I'm entitled to take it without anyone's permission and without a single shred of doubt about the rights and wrongs of it. I could see no reason why she could begrudge me it given that my need was greater although I felt sure she would probably find one. I put the radio on to drown out the raking sound of the windscreen wipers and turned the radio up to full blast all the way down to the coast. The rain lashed down harder than ever, bouncing off the tarmac and reducing the visibility to a few rear lights glowing in the middle lane ahead. I don't know about you, but I've always felt as though it's a race to the sea. I'm always anxious to get there, to see the first signs of land meeting water. I was content to drive like this for hours until I eventually began to notice the signs for my turn off through the deluge. As the downpour began to ease I casually pulled over into the inside lane to get ready to leave at the next junction. Just as I began to steer to the left I was cut up by a BMW racing to get ahead of me across the chevrons and nearly ploughing into the rising grassy embankment on the right. Instinctively I hit the brake pedal and only just managed to pull further into the left lane to avoid him. I punched my horn at the bastard. His brake lights came on and we both crawled to a standstill at the roundabout. He indicated that he wanted to pull over. An arm appeared from the window and beckoned me to follow him until we had pulled into a residential street just off one the main roads. I parked several car lengths behind him and waited for him to get out. I could see the two of them through his rear window. He seemed to be saying something to his wife or girlfriend. I opened my door cautiously and walked towards the front to check for any damage. I crouched down to touch the wet bumper with my fingers before looking back at the driver. The rain was blowing against my face and I felt it beginning to soak into my thighs. As he approached I shielded my eyes to get a better look. He was a handsome man, bald and well built, wearing an incongruous pair of yellow ski-ing goggles, a grey shirt and a long black leather jacket. He looked not much older than forty. He came towards me with both arms outstretched as if it was all a big misunderstanding.

'What did you think you were doing?' I said

He made a cursory glance towards my car.

'I'm so sorry. I hope there isn't much damage?' he asked. His accent was European but I couldn't pin it down.

'That's not the point. You could have killed us.'

'I'm really sorry. I totally underestimated the speed required to overtake you in this rain. It was my fault. Please allow me to give you my details.'

I wasn't sure what else there was to say. In my previous

life I might have flipped into a rage. In my previous life I would have cared far too much about all of this. Instead I followed him back to his car.

'What's up with your girlfriend? Is she in shock?'

He smiled and shook his head.

'Please take a look for yourself. She's OK.'

I walked round to the passenger side and looked in. His girlfriend, if you could call her that, was pale and motionless. She was naked from the waist down. Her dark brown eyes and long eyelashes pointed straight ahead and she wore a pale, thin smile. Her owner had covered her head with a blonde wig and a broad black hat. He'd clothed her upper body in a winter coat.

'She's very tasteful,' I said, 'If a little inappropriately dressed for the weather.'

'So glad you like her,' said the man, 'Let me get a pen and paper for you.'

He opened the driver's side and leaned over to the glove compartment which immediately fell off as soon as he opened it.

'I hope you don't find this abrupt but why do you drive around with a mannequin?'

'Why not?' replied the man still rummaging around for a pen.

'You're the first person I've met who does.'

He scrambled back through the door bumping his head on the roof of the car as he tried to repair the glove compartment and put it back in place.

'Here you are. My number and address and you have my number plates.'

I took the scrap of paper from him. His name was Nikola Petrov, a resident of the same city we were both heading for.

'I'm not sure what you want me to say. I can't see any damage. I don't think we made contact.'

'Just in case you want to make contact,' he said and

handed the note to me. I had a few scraps of paper in my wallet and, shielding the paper against the wind and rain, I noted down my details before handing the pen and paper back to him.

'Thank you,' he said, 'Now if you are ok you must excuse me. It's raining and I am late for a conference.'

He pulled his leather coat around himself and climbed back into the car.

'Drive carefully,' I said before he had a chance to shut the door.

'Thank you. I will,' he replied.

I bent over to stare at him through the window. Now that I look back on it I could swear that I saw him pat his companion on the thigh before setting off or was he just reaching for the handbrake?

It was mid-day when I arrived in the city. I drove towards the sea, pulling into a car park not far from the Aquarium. A group of children in cheap plastic rain protectors jogged past, squealing at the rain as they raced ahead of their parents to get to the sharks and stingrays. I spent a long time with the windscreen wipers off, staring at the sea, knowing full well that I had to get moving to have any hope of getting myself into the flat that night. But I couldn't move. I rummaged around for a sandwich that I'd bought on the way down and watched the rain water beating down on the windscreen. Through the windows I could make out the surface of the dark sea rolling in. Or was it rolling out? I watched the sea for a while trying to figure out which way it was going. This procrastination astonishes me now that I can see what it is. A sharp knock on the window of the driver's side startled me. It was someone trying to get into the car parked next to mine. Then my phone started buzzing and vibrating in my coat pocket. It was Helen.

'What the hell you think you're doing?' she began

'What do you mean?' I said.

'What gives you the right to take off like that? That was

my car.'

'I bought it. You can buy a new one yourself.'

'That still doesn't give you the right.'

'…hang on…'

'You should have told me that you were moving out this week. Some of us have got plans you know. I needed it this weekend for something the girls have got planned. We're going to a spa in Kent. How am I supposed to get there?'

'…..wait…..'

'I want the car back on Friday and you can take the train back.'

She hung up.

I got out of the car, walked across the tarmac and onto the pebble beach, battling through the wind and rain until I reached the sea and steadied myself to throw the damn phone into the crashing waves. I couldn't. It remained in the palm of my hand and I couldn't part with it. I couldn't cut myself off even when faced with the most unfeeling provocation. I began to notice people around me and I walked back to the car and started the engine. It wasn't long before I'd parked up outside Matilda's office. One of her colleagues recognized me as soon as I walked in.

'Matilda has a day off,' he said, 'She'll be back tomorrow.'

'OK… I've come to collect the keys.'

'Er….OK…sure,' he said and jogged to the back of the office to open up a cupboard. He returned with a set of keys and a map with directions to the flat, some vouchers for a few of the shops in the area and a brochure about some local events.

'Thanks. And thank Matilda for me. She found me a great place.'

I left feeling a bit disappointed that Matilda hadn't been there. I needed to see a friendly face to replenish myself in spite of the horrors of the day.

I spent the rest of the afternoon buying a few items for

the flat; a blow-up mattress, a kettle, some plates, cutlery and a set of cheap pots and pans. I shopped around for bedding but in all honesty I would have been happy to buy an over priced hipster duvet cover if it looked functional and clean. I chose one that depicted the massive face of a llama or alpaca wearing big shades. They were the same colour of yellow shades that I saw Nikola Petrov wearing. It felt appropriate. Later, when I dragged it all back to the flat and breathed in the smell of fresh polish I paced the wooden floors, inspecting every room again and again. In the kitchen I opened all the cupboard doors, peering into them and admiring their empty spaces. There was something beautiful about it, like leaving home for the first time. I took a few pictures and posted them online.

It had stopped raining. I opened one of the lounge windows to listen to the sounds of the street outside then pumped up the mattress and lay on it for a while, staring at the white walls and ceiling. By now, feeling quite content with everything, I had an urge to phone my family to let them know where I was. The flat was equipped with a small sofa and so I sat down and began dialling but I had second thoughts. I hadn't the heart to tell them. Nor was I prepared to burn every possible way back to Helen. She might change her mind after this strange fling of hers fizzles out. It might turn out to be a psychological illness or crisis and it's perfectly possible that she might emerge from it and we look back on it in years to come as a strange interruption in our relationship. It didn't take long for a few messages to appear in response to my update on the flat. Mum first.

'Can't talk now mum. Bit tired after all that work moving in. Say hello to Dad. Love R xxxxx.'

I had message from my sister. The bold opening line *'Relationship Status???????'* didn't bode well.

'Don't worry,' I replied, *'I saw that too. No panico. Just a glitch in the Matrix. H being rubbish with technology.'*

I clicked on the screen showing the full roster of my

friends and their profile pictures. Helen was still there but she'd strengthened her security settings to block me from browsing her personal pages. The ticker that counts the number of connections I have had dropped a notch. I braced myself for a further drop in my social stocks and shares over the coming months.

As evening arrived I had the urge to eat a banquet. Rather than spend my first evening alone the prospect of seeing the city at night was too tempting to resist, so I grabbed my camera and stepped out into the twilight. I have to say that I've been overwhelmed by the freshness of my surroundings. I took photographs of things that I wouldn't normally have thought of as significant, registering my environment like an android in an alien world.

Indian lady and husband working late in the pharmacy. Click.

A Jack Russell tied to a lamppost outside a convenience shop. Click.

Motorcycles parked outside a seafront fishmongers. Click.

Lone white bouncer standing outside empty pub with disco lights circling the floor. Click.

Retro posters for upcoming air show. Click.

After half a mile or so I found myself in a street lined with restaurants and began processing the type of cuisine on offer when I had an idea. Look up the reviews. My phone brought up several of them with varying recommendations and trashings of the different establishments on offer. The funny thing was that it in no way helped me to make a balanced decision and if anything I remained firmly on track to head for the first one I could see within a short distance of where I was standing and which looked modern and had a few decent reviews. People do this all the time when they respond to information especially when prompted by instinct so why would I feel any different? Inside a graceful Thai waitress showed me to a small table by one of the walls. I sat down and began reading the menu. Once you order there is not much else to do in a restaurant when you're dining alone but cast your eyes over your fellow diners to weigh up their possible lives. I chose very quickly. I then tapped in the restaurant name and brought up the reviews while I waited. Odd how things work out and perhaps too strangle for words was a review by NikkiPetrov. Not *the* NikkiPetrov surely? How many of them can there be in this city? It begins:

Combines all the charm of an empty corporate boardroom with modest Thai food

I watched the tables fill up with people until the restaurant was filled with the tap and hum of conversation, both real and virtual. I felt an inexplicable pressure to get up and leave but forced myself to stay.

The review continued:

If you have tasted good home cooking in Thailand you'll know that aromatic and simple dishes of food are what you expect from a restaurant like this. Not so here. The food is OK as far as it goes. Some re-inventor of the genre has decided to divest the way that Thai food can evoke joy and pleasure like its bamboo furniture and motor scooters to replace it with a dreary binary fusion of white tables, black chairs and dimmed electric lights that remind one of staying at a lonely airport hotel.

Such is the immense weight of social expectations that an experience is only a valuable experience if it is shared. It's not sufficient to think a thought without acting as though someone else might benefit from reading it. I took some solace in reading a journalist's column about the rapid spread of online rage on the pages of social media. My two courses arrived quickly, the waitress smiled at me each time she approached my table and the whole room buzzed and hummed with the excited conversation and laughter of dozens of people. The food was Ok but better than I'd expected after reading the review. It was too tempting not to respond to Petrov's review with a rebuttal.

Food. Enjoyable. Service. Prompt and Friendly. Atmosphere. Buzzing.

In one swift journey, in one day, I have made it to the other side of my existence. I have arrived in a place that might as well have been named 'Nowhere'. It might still be a Utopia for all I know. It's one thing to pull off the feat of escaping from my former life but quite another to arrive in a new one. Adapting to the new environment hasn't been all that difficult so far. There is still so much in London that might tug me back but if I had wanted to remain it was only a matter of time before a new life would have come looking for me. So here's the thing, as Tony Blair used to say. After the meal I walked into the nearest bar for a drink. Inside, the air seemed heavy with the scent of sweat and perfume. People were gathered round tables, laughing, gesticulating, nodding and shouting to each other. Standing at the end of the bar, I had the perfect shot of the rows of men waiting for their drinks. They wore their attitudes like armbands. Those with muscle stared like big cats, others smiled through their tanned faces like devils, some waved notes in the air and howled with impatience as another opportunity passed them by. The picture was ready made. All I had to do was frame it and so I drew my camera out of my shoulder bag and snapped away.

'No photography allowed,' said a female voice.

I turned around to see two pretty young things standing just behind me waiting for a space to appear at the bar; a powerfully build blonde and a tall girl with a friendly smile and a large gap between her two front teeth.

'And why not?' I asked.

'Because it's the rules. Haven't you heard it's rude to take pictures of people without their permission,' said the blonde one.

'Do I have your permission?'

They put their arms around each other. The tall one threw her shoulders and hair back and the other girl began to make a movie-star pout.

'Do you want it?' I said.

'Let me see,' said the blonde one.

I turned the camera around to display the image.

'It's a great one of you honey.'

'Are you going to put it on the screen?' asked the tall one, indicating a flat screen television behind me.

'No, not exactly. I'm an artist. A creative. I don't work here.'

'Then what are you going to do with it? Why are you taking pictures?' she went on.

'I do it for art. For building up a portfolio of work.'

'But you've got our image now. How do *we* know what you're going to do with it?'

'I'll delete it. Or send it to your phone. Honestly it's not a big deal for me.'

The girls looked at each other and smiled.

'I suppose that's one way of getting a girl's number. You're not a psychopath are you?' asked the blonde.

By now things were starting to feel a little weird and I could sense some of the men behind the bar taking an interest in what might be happening. But the girls' curiosity had peaked and within seconds they dismissed me with a 'Byeeeeee!' and pushed their way in amongst the rows of men.

To be 'Nowhere' and 'No-one'. Which of those twins would you rather hang out with? What if you had to hold hands with both of them?

I've made my first foray into this new territory and have discovered for the first time that I have lost something in my years with Helen. I had been living under the illusion that I am still an attractive man. I never thought of myself as especially handsome, but I did believe I was attractive enough if you know what I mean. There had always been a worrying thought at the back of my mind during all those years of the relationship that saw Helen, not as the only perfect lover and companion, but as someone amongst many other bright and attractive women I could have appealed to if needed. It doesn't feel like that now. As I walked around the bar and bumped into groups of men and women I became aware of how oblivious they were of my existence and how deluded I had been to go along with Anders view that another relationship might be easy to obtain. As I returned home and reached my front door I noticed a dull light emanating from the other side. I thought for a moment that someone might have been there and put my head against the door to listen. There was nothing to suggest someone moving around the flat. I pressed on and opened the door to find the glare of a laptop screen that I must have left on all the while I was out. The online world beckoned, and I landed on a dating site by no small or strange co-incidence. Quite a number of female profiles warned players and psychos not to message them as if both archetypes have ever bothered to consider what anyone else thought. I took the liberty of taking Hare's Psychopathy Test and scored an overall percentage of 27%. Surprisingly low I thought. I posted the score to my social media account and for the first time in my life considered buying 500ml of oxytocin nasal spray, a banner ad for which had started to appear in the margins of my web browser.

5.

Like any explorer I have been a mixture of curiosity and desperation since I last posted. You didn't think I would give up at the first attempt did you? So what if this new world is a little hostile to begin with. Isn't that always the way? It feels natural at this point to explore my surroundings online as well as the physical space around me. Isn't that what the pre-millennial pioneers of being online meant with their fledgling communities and attempts to map the route to Utopia? And despite this or even because of the early founding fathers it seems as though we are all true descendants of the Fourierists and have grown used to trading and bartering outside the system, in self-improvement, liberated sex and free expression. No need to build a bricks and mortar *phalanstere* for all the different social classes to mingle. We are all living in a virtual *phalanstere* now. Like any good utopian I realised that the best way to enter a new community was to have something to offer. I've knocked up a website offering my services as a photographer. A few portraits of models and glamorous shots of women in spectacular landscapes from my advertising days and I'm up and running. Like a true bargain hunter I've managed to find a home for recycled furniture and slowly but surely the flat is going to fill up with some unusual pieces from the 1960's. I've also set to work on setting aside one of the bedrooms as the studio where I thought I might be able to do some low-key private work if needed. I can see the apartment taking on the appearance of a creative space from the Witchetty Grub if I'm not careful.

Even so, the problem of how to fill the days remains. Helen hasn't been in touch and I can't think of anything to say to her after our last row. Curiously I feel nothing for her. It's as though she has never existed. Is that difficult to understand? Perhaps because it doesn't seem possible that you can go from loving someone to no longer caring about them at all. It's dangerous and disturbing even. But as I no longer see her my subconscious mind seems to have taken it as read that she has gone from reality as if she were a character in an online game. She might as well have never existed. And I don't find it shocking to write those words. Can five years of our relationship, our love be discarded and erased so easily? Yes is the answer. Yes they can and much more besides. So more out of curiosity than any residual affection I dropped her a line to see if she was willing to talk. Several days passed and I got no response. I was neither disappointed or surprised, just curious as to how the affair was going. Was she still with him? Who is he and how did they meet? When and where did it all begin? The one thing that I have in abundance is time, large swollen reservoirs of time that no longer seem to have a purpose. After living with Helen for so many years I hadn't realised how many hours filled up a typical day. When there's no noise a day can be an endless stretch, a beautiful stretch of time to inhabit. It stands like an empty wine glass waiting to be filled and there were times when I've filled it with enough of the Pisco to nudge me to the end.

Some old friends from the Witchetty Grub dropped by to cheer me up, promising, like the good souls they are, to pass me some work but we spent more time talking about my new surroundings. Typically, it was Charles who got straight to the issue.

'Shame about Helen. We all feel gutted for you. But are you sure this is this the right place for you? Out here. Sea air and all that. Might be good for the soul but are you ready to take it all on? Why not come back?'

'No thanks, I'm doing alright for myself, even if there's bugger all work out here. I feel great. I mean healthy. Out here I can think, breathe, come up with new ideas,' I heard myself reply without really feeling party to the words.

'Spoken like the great optimist. You always were like that even after a shambolic client presentation.'

That was unexpected. I hadn't realised I was seen as that kind of person.

'One of *your* client presentations Charles,' chipped in Suzanna.

'Yes. Indeed. But seriously now Rich. How *are* you getting on with your new artistic vision?' Charles continued.

'The artistic vision? Well, I'm still visualizing it for want of a better phrase.'

'So you haven't done anything yet.'

'Yes, pretty much.'

Laughter all round and Charles goes off to buy another round of drinks.

The truth is I do have a few ideas, but I get the impression that they wouldn't make sense to my former colleagues. I want to document real people, draw out the raw variety of their personalities and emotions. When I look inside my own soul I can't detect anything left to feel. Around me I can see people bristling with emotion. I suspect that none of it will be of any commercial value but that doesn't concern me. I've done enough commercial work to last me a lifetime and I already know everything anyone could ever need to know about what it takes to shift a product.

The first opportunity I had to realise my new artistic enterprise happened quite by accident only a week later. The Annual Airshow by the beach promised to showcase some classic aircraft from the twentieth century with a Lancaster bomber and Spitfires promised as the highlights. I took the Nikon to the beach in the hope of being able to take some pictures. It was a hot June day. The seafront was packed with kids and their parents. In this temporary theatre by the sea where the toddler rubs noses with the Staffordshire Bull

Terrier, where the divorced father hugs his kids close, I watched the distant throbbing planes which bring everyone's hands to their foreheads to glimpse the approaching bomber. I began to snap away. Not so much at the Lancaster but the faces in the crowd. I crouched to get a better glimpse of their faces against the backdrop of the sky. The bomber was soon over our heads and the expressions of some fell as the noise of the engines finally caught up and its shadow glided elegantly below us. The bomber passed over, flying at low altitude, close enough to get a good look at the marks on the undercarriage. I moved further down the seafront and closer to the pier where a DJ had set up with loudspeakers. His commentary on the pilots and their planes crackled over the beach as the Lancaster was followed by another aeronautics display. As the next set of planes began to appear as dots in the distance I got a shot of a few teenage girls who were kicking a ball around on the beach.

'Ahoy there Mr. Photographer,' said a voice behind me.

I turned around and pointed the camera in the direction of the voice.

'Well hello,' I said, 'I didn't think airshows would be your thing.'

It was Matilda, no longer wearing her ill-fitting navy suit but white knee length trousers and a pink shirt tied at the waist. She wore an Alice band and her sunglasses were perched on the end of her nose like telescopic ray guns.

'That's what you think,' she went on, 'I happen to like a good loop the loop. Do you like the Red Arrows?…..my Dad used to take me to see them when I was a kid.'

'It's very old fashioned but interesting.'

'And how are you and girlfriend getting on in the flat? No regrets leaving London?'

'No, the flat's wonderful but she's decided not to come with me. And no, I don't have any regrets.'

'I see.'

Matilda joined me on the pebbled beach and pushed her glasses back to the bridge of her nose.

'Well?' she asked.

'Well what?'

'What's next Photographer Man?'

'Pretend I'm not here.'

Matilda ignored me and clapped her hands excitedly.

'Loop the loop! Yay!' she yelled.

The DJ announced the arrival of the next aircraft, a Canadian Harvard, which had already begun its ascent into the loop it was about to perform. I snapped away at the fighter as it chugged upwards and then turned my lens towards Matilda. I zoomed in on her face capturing her freckles and tilted nose then turned my attention back towards the crowds of people around us. There he was. The mannequin man. Was that his dummy standing beside him? He had his arm around a young blonde, taller than him and about the same age as Matilda. She was real enough, and Petrov seemed to play along obliging me by pulling his girl closer to him and leaning in for a prolonged kiss. I didn't want to pry and turned back to Matilda. She was jumping up and down and yelling at me.

'Wow. Did you see that? He was so close to skimming the sea. Watch this one. He's doing it again.'

I was still more interested in the crowd. I was enjoying their rapture at what they were seeing and increased the shutter speed to capture this blissful moment surfacing on their cheeks and in the crows' feet around their eyes. They raised their chins and smiled in unison as the Harvard climbed for another loop. As it pitched downwards I kept my focus on their faces, including Matilda's. But something wasn't quite right. She raised her fingers to her mouth. Someone screamed. Matilda looked at me and then the sea and wagged a finger at the camera. The DJ had stopped the music. I lowered the Nikon for a second and stared at the horizon. There, floating on the surface of the water were a

49

few scraps of materials, part of a wing or a tail fin. A circle of foam had been churned up on the surface, buffeting these fragments in different directions. A lifeboat was already ploughing its way through the water to examine the wreckage and any sign of the pilot. Matilda leaned into me and I put my arm around her shoulder.

No-one spoke. The sound of the lifeboat engine drifted on the breeze. All was quiet until the boat arrived at the scene of the wreck. A diver rolled backwards into the water and began his rescue. No-one moved. I took what pictures I could of the crowd, the bits of wreckage on the surface, hoping that they might form the background to a more miraculous story of the diver emerging with a survivor, but I think we all knew this wasn't going to happen. We waited, still wanting to believe that what we had witnessed was unreal or that it could still be made whole in the end. Before long, as the wait for the diver's return seemed to drag on interminably the noise of people talking began to simmer in the air. 'I can't believe what just happened. Did he misjudge it? Was it suicide? I wonder where his family are? I just can't believe it' and so on, everyone repeating the same phrases over again. Matilda was dumbstruck. She cried as the diver emerged from the water and seemed to shake his head. Was that a negative? Or just the cold water that made him shiver?

She looked at me shaking her head.

'He didn't make it. He couldn't have,' she said.

'No, there's nothing we can do. I don't feel comfortable watching this anymore, but I feel as though we owe it to him to see it through.'

'Me too.'

She buried her head in my chest and I knew what was expected of me. I had to console her. This would bring about the right response, restore some faith in common humanity. So I did, knowing full well that it was necessary of me to play the role. Let me make this clear. I didn't do it because I felt anything apart from shock; something I'm getting very familiar with now. I was genuinely sorry for the poor man, but I also found myself thinking, 'men die all the time and we don't spare them a thought'. Somewhere, in a hospital ward there's a man screaming with pain. Is anyone watching? Something was missing in my reactions. I expected to feel more and was frustrated that I couldn't, but I knew what the situation required and fulfilled it to the best of my ability.

We walked to an empty bar nearby. The landlord had run outside to see what all the fuss was about and was sheltering his eyes from the sun and looking out to sea. An ambulance raced past us, sirens blaring and wailing, towards the beach. We passed the stricken landlord and stumbled our way up a rickety old staircase to a balcony on the upper storey looking out to sea. Matilda was still shaking as I led her to a seat. I thought I might be able to snap her out of it and reached out to touch her gently on the arm.

'How are you feeling now?'

'Depressed,' she said, 'No not depressed. That's not the right word. I mean it's horrible. I can't stop thinking about it. Do you find that?'

'Yes. Look. There are videos of the crash on social media.'

'Already?'

'Yes, there's one here that was quite near us.'

Matilda leaned in and we watched the death loop again, the sudden intakes of breath, the silence and shouts of 'Oh my God!' And there as the camera swooped around we caught a glimpse of ourselves. Briefly frozen in time and then gone.

'Oh. I've got to tell people I'm OK,' she said, and the look of concern gradually fell away from her face and as she retrieved the phone from her handbag it was replaced by one of total concentration.

I retrieved my phone then put it to one side. I could see

the script and knew its lines all too well and could predict what she was probably typing. I waited in silence for her to share her story. This was undoubtedly a tragedy for the pilot so what purpose was there in adding to the world's stock of how other people felt about it? Would it console anyone? I didn't feel consoled and waited a full ten minutes or so for her to reply to the buzzing of messages on her phone. Eventually it was Matilda who resumed the conversation.

'I'm not really meant to be selling property,' she said as she typed something into her phone without looking up, 'I've got a degree in archaeology. I should be doing something else with my life, digging the soil or teaching but I've got used to the money here. And I love the sea.'

'What about your family?'

She stopped typing and looked up at me.

'Oh them. I still live at home with them. It's nice to have them around but I should move out really.'

'Well why not? You could do it easily.'

Matilda just shrugged her shoulders and put her phone down.

'Lots of reasons. Too complicated to go into now.'

She shook her head.

'No, it's OK. They're saying that the pilot used to be in the RAF. He has a daughter the same age as me. I can't believe it. It's so, so sad. Look, let's talk about you. What happened? I thought you and your girlfriend were starting a new life.'

'We were. We still are in a way,' I said, and we began talking it over. She listened attentively despite my clumsy way of explaining what had happened. For the first time I felt awkward about it as if it would be impossible for anyone else to understand. I didn't understand it myself. It's a hard thing to sustain, this dance of revealing yourself slowly to someone else, and I didn't feel comfortable with it. Not in person anyway. I would have been more than happy to type it but to say it was a different matter. I became aware of

Matilda's looks as she nodded and frowned at different aspects of my story. She looked as though she genuinely cared.

'Sounds like a bitch. You had a lucky escape,' she said.

I couldn't be sure if her reactions were the result of some subterfuge on my part but that seemed absurd. Was I laying it on too thick or were these spontaneous reactions from Matilda genuine? What I did next was to stop speaking just to see what would happen. As soon as I did I realised that she would probably think that I might be suppressing something. She reached out and stroked my arm very gently until she reached my hand with the tips of her fingers. It seems to me that the best way to reduce pain is to share in its universal appeal, tell a joke about it, or simply to touch someone. I felt as though I'd given a bad performance. Matilda was giving a very good one.

'You don't have to explain anything to me. I know what you're going through,' she said.

'I don't quite feel able to grasp it,' I said, 'I feel more like a robot than a man.'

Matilda leaned in to give me a peck on the cheek.

'You're not a machine,' she said, 'I should know.'

We drank up and left the bar moving onto another and then another and I felt myself being taken back years to the days when my capacity for drinking was as weak and feeble as my artistic ambitions and any admiration I received from women was snatched in moments of complete inebriation.

6.

Internet Browsing History for 17th July

8.06 - Centre for European Studies - Nikola Petrov
8.09 - Google Scholar - Paralelismo? What is it?
8.36 - Iwona - porn directory #12
8.46 - Iwona releases debut novel to mixed reviews
8.58 - Dalahar called before House Select Committee - The Times

There is an alternative time zone that anyone connected with the online world inhabits. It's as if one's body is simultaneously travelling steadily across one latitude whilst the mind is airborne and circling the earth at a different speed entirely. I thought I'd commit some of my Internet browsing history to the journal to illustrate the point. As I began to copy and paste, I made a small discovery. The browsing history itself is another journal, an alternative thought record, to the one I'm writing. I find, when I look back on it, that it runs in parallel to the more menial task of recollecting events and people. I've included it here to hint at some of the seemingly spontaneous topics that I have been typing into search engines. But are they spontaneous or do they follow a predetermined trajectory? I hesitate to include everything but as the almost gravitational pull of the robot in me grows stronger I wonder if I will ever be able to resist it.

A whole week has passed since Matilda and I spent the night together. Then, out of nowhere her photo popped up on my phone with a message. I still have the chain of instant messages.

'Hi, how are u?'

'Hi, I'm good. How are you feeling?'

'Are u around today? A friend's having a house warming. Wanna come?'

'Sorry honey. I've got one or two things to do in London.'

'Ok, up to you. Message me later if u r coming.'

I can't think why I was so disengaged. The truth was that I'd also been browsing the Internet for events where I might be able to take pictures of crowds. The newspapers had run with one of my pictures from the Airshow. Significantly, it wasn't one of the crash but of the horrified and shocked expressions of the spectators. The event marked something of a breakthrough. As I sifted through the images I knew that I'd hit on something I wanted to explore. This was raw emotion. These reactions to the plane crash were not scripted. There were no masks on display here and no manipulation of emotional responses. I'd had enough of all that from company directors, all striving to elicit the right reaction, with their armies of communications specialists. I wanted the real reaction, the reaction of the people. I printed out the images including the ones of Petrov posing with his girlfriend and Matilda with her sunglasses and stuck them up all over the walls of the second bedroom. She looked an absolute peach. I had wanted to see Matilda and had almost sent her a message a couple of times but something about our parting the morning after our night together made me reconsider. She woke up first. As I began to come round I noticed her sitting on the end of the bed hunched over her phone. She was texting someone. Her reactions were as cold as a snake, her face was lifeless and she could hardly bring herself to smile.

She didn't stick around for long, preferring to skip breakfast and get back to her place. 'Call me,' she said as she left. It wasn't exactly inviting and so the sudden enthusiasm to go with her to a party, presumably to be given the seal of approval by her young friends, seemed like a naff option.

I preferred to get on with some work and looked around at the pictures on the walls. Even now, as I take myself back to the day of the crash, I can still feel something. For a brief moment, if I close my eyes, I feel the rush of adrenalin in my veins. I looked at Petrov's picture again. I want to know more about this man. I squandered a few idle hours looking him up. The name Nikola Petrov brought up instant results and it didn't take long for me to identify the man with the mannequin. His profession was listed as Lecturer in Online Communications at the city's university. He'd been there since 2010 and had built up quite an online presence. He ran courses on the psychology of self-actualization and collective consciousness, whatever that means. He'd left his imprint all over the city in the comments sections of newspapers and online communities and even in all the city's online restaurant reviews. Reading several of them he evidently thought nothing of sampling and commenting on the most expensive bottles on the wine list. Naturally he had his own website and blogged on everything from the war against terror to the issue of European integration. He had his own Twitter following. Over five hundred people followed his titbits of information. Curiously they seemed to be a little obscure. Reading through them was a disorientating experience. He seemed to be writing coded messages to his followers although I wasn't sure if it might also have been his accent.

'Sometimes you have to go into the reverse gear before you can get moving on the road,' was one such tweet to one of his acolytes.

'Friends. Bring me your stories and make them happen!' was one of many exhortations.

I could find no mention of the mannequin I'd seen him with in the car or the blonde model I'd photographed him with on the beach. He'd had some professional photographs taken for his websites and no doubt they answered his need to look every inch the European intellectual; grizzled, asexual and bald. Yet the paradox seems to me that as much as he criticised it he had no quarrel with many aspects of the modern world in either his eclectic online presence or his preference for self-promotion. Below his profile I noticed a blank box for sending messages and filled it in with a greeting and a cock and bull story about wanting to photograph him for a magazine article.

I clicked 'send' and turned away from the screen to make a coffee. The phone rang.

I ignored it, worried that it might be Helen. A few seconds later it went off again. It was Mum. I put the phone in a drawer and went back to my desk. There was a reply from him. I clicked on it eagerly, but I needn't have been so keen.

'Thank you for your enquiry and for taking an interest in my work. I am away at the moment and will respond to you on my return. In the meantime why not take a look at my latest voluntary project. Let me know if you'd be willing to participate. See you on the other side. Nik.'

See you on the other side?

That image of Petrov's blonde girlfriend taken at the airshow reminded me that despite Matilda's attention I was still alone. I rode the Internet searching out ways to make myself happy. If I pulled up all my browsing history I could probably tell you how many hours I spent in the world of MILFs and lesbians, candy crushes and one YouTube playlist after another. It sounds like a circus but if anything I've very quickly got into a settled routine of indulging in this dubious of all benefits of the Internet.

But I've also had to get down to some work. Anders has been in touch since my move to the sea. He lined up some freelance work for me for a lottery-funded charity. I took him up on the offer and several days later found myself travelling up on the train to meet him in the Docklands and then on to the New Den in Millwall. It was another opportunity to sit with crowds and monitor their sprawling emotions. The air crash was too morbid on its own and I felt I needed to keep adding to this theme of crowds and their emotions. On the journey up to London I opened up my tablet and began watching a film. Half-way through I received a message from Helen. It really feels as though she's installed a tracking app on my devices. 'We need to talk. Can u meet me in Charing Cross?' she said.

I suspected a reconciliation. It didn't sound like Helen. Did she know that I had forgotten about our relationship already and couldn't bear to allow me to forget? But of course I'd got into the habit of announcing my movements in social media. All those wasted evenings checking the career moves of porn actresses now came into sharp focus and I couldn't for the life of me remember why I hadn't done more research into my property rights when I still had the time. Helen, on the other hand, would almost certainly be prepared and so I agreed reluctantly to the meeting. I was too curious about Helen not to go and, as this was the first sign she had given that she still possessed a pulse since I moved away, I agreed. There was more than enough time to kill before the match kicked off. An hour later I was waiting in a café underneath St Martin-in-the-Fields, trying to work out what I was going to do. I wasn't sure how to act. I still felt anaesthetised as if I was the go-between for the real man she'd cheated on. A number of responses seemed to present themselves. I could get upset if I knew how to. I thought about whether I could fake it but then why make myself pitiable? I suspected that Helen would break down in tears at some point if only to help deflect her guilt onto me. It didn't seem a very realistic or dignified way forward. I could get angry, but I'd been down that route before and I hadn't any anger left. I could pretend that I had moved on with my life and although true to a certain extent it didn't really ring true. That's the thing. We are the walking adverts of our lives. People really want the truth but more than that they really want things to seem true and that's not the same thing. It's not enough for the facts to add up. All of this took up lots of precious time that I might have used to plan what to say and before I knew it she had crept up behind me like a school teacher and was standing at my shoulder.

'I can't stay long,' she said, 'I've got an appointment at two.'

'Well you can't miss that obviously,' I said without thinking.

'Are you going to be like that?' she said, and I noticed she wasn't willing at this point even to make eye contact.

'Like what? This is a little bit strange for me. It must be for you too.'

'I can't sleep. You know how I used to have a reaction to sleeping pills.'

I remembered her numerous addictions but not the reactions. I said nothing.

She pulled her handbag up to her lap and then slumped into her chair, shoulders bent in. Then she puffed her cheeks and looked directly into my eyes.

'Oh, look at you. I can't decide whether to give you a hug or not.'

'I'm fine,' I said.

'I thought it important that we had some time away from each other. To reflect on things.'

'Yes.'

'I mean, it's been horrible for both of us, and you must have felt absolutely awful. It's not the way I wanted things to work out. You probably find that ridiculous but honestly it wasn't. I couldn't let you down gently without being deceitful. The longer it continued the worse it would have been for you and you wouldn't have appreciated that. It doesn't make sense to go on pretending. You would have sensed something was wrong. I wasn't avoiding you. I know that's what you were probably thinking. I couldn't speak to you because I was in bits. I couldn't stop myself crying. It was the only way I could tell you.'

I could see her eyes begin to well up with tears.

'Don't cry,' I said and waited for her to gather her emotions together.

'No, it's OK. I could do with a good cry. I'm feeling so much more emotional all the time.'

'Where are you living at the moment? I mean are you on your own?'

'I can't go back to the flat. That's what I wanted to say to you. I'm going to have to rent it out. If you want to take something you'd better let me know. There's still loads of your stuff there and you can't expect me to deal with it. If you don't come and collect it in the next couple of weeks I'm sending it to charity. Or you can put it into storage. It's up to you.'

'Wait. You haven't given me a chance to think about this.'

'You've had plenty of time Rich. You chose to abandon everything and run off. You've got the car.'

'I paid for that car.'

'We both used it if you remember. I have a right to it as much as you do. And another thing, just because you don't live there any more it doesn't mean you don't have to pay the bills. I want half the bills transferred to our joint account for the last two months Rich.'

'Fine. I'll do it. I'll do it. Look I've been very stressed out about this. I think we need to talk about selling it.'

'I'm not prepared to do that. I need time.'

'What happened to you Helen? Did you meet someone else?'

She seized up, 'So it's my fault is it?'

'Don't be like that. This is the first time I've been able to ask you about it.'

'Really? So you didn't hang up on me or refuse to return any of my calls?

I kept my mouth shut.

'You didn't see it happening?' she asked.

'I was happy. I thought we both were. Why else would we plan a life away from London together? Why did you let me book all those viewings?'

'Our relationship had faded away Rich. After the miscarriage I started to feel different. You seemed quite content to carry on as normal as if nothing had happened. I couldn't do that, but I didn't want to hold you back. I wanted to have children. What would have been the point of trying to make it work if we didn't feel the same? I knew it wouldn't work anymore.'

'We never talked about it.'

'You didn't feel the need to.'

Helen fished around some clutter in her handbag and drew out a black leather-bound notebook.

'Do you realise how much it costs to raise a child? I mean to raise a child properly and give them a chance in life. If I opt to have children I'm going to have to give up work for a while or go part-time and I need someone to support me. Food, nappies, car seats, buggies, cot, clothes, books, toys, childcare, school and nursery fees. You name it. It's expensive. Look it up.'

'I had a good job. I could have helped.'

'And what are you doing now?'

'I'm making a living as a photographer. Ok. It's not much but it's just enough to cover the rent.'

'I needed more security than that Rich.'

'I could have given you that. I could get a job back in London right now if I wanted to. My ads speak for themselves.'

'I'm sorry but it's too late. I've met someone.'

We hadn't spoken for over six weeks and now she couldn't stop.

'I've known him for a long time, from years ago. Before I met you. Then we split up and never really spoke to one another. Now we've reconnected. We met up again for the first time last weekend so you needn't worry. I wasn't seeing anyone behind your back.'

I was reeling from the double-edged sword that was Helen's conviction that I wasn't a suitable father and could be replaced with a more suitable candidate. I hadn't realised that there was a secret recruitment process in place. She sounds convincing doesn't she, but I knew that she and this other guy had probably been fucking each other for some time.

'Are you listening?' said Helen.

'Yes.'

'Well?'

'I…..what do you expect me to say to that?'

'Have it your way,' Helen went on, 'It doesn't make any difference. If you want to play it rough then two can play at that game. I think I've said what I needed to say and unless you have anything more to say I'll wait to hear from you about picking up your things.'

With that she left her cappuccino untouched and walked away. As she turned towards the exit and her face re-emerged from behind one of the arches supporting the crypt I thought I might just get one last shot of her with my Nikon. I caught her as she hurried away and checked the digital display for any sign of emotion. On the second of the two pictures I thought I noticed something and zoomed in to take a closer look. Her face was in profile and she was looking downwards. I followed the line of her vision towards the notebook and the fingers wrapped around it. It was then that I noticed a new ring on her left hand. It seemed that the war for my soul was well and truly underway as it is for so many. We have a usefulness like coal or gas that lasts as long as we continue to burn but one day our all too finite resources will dry up and what then? I had no intention of giving up and going back to London and nothing Helen could say would change my mind.

I packed up my things and headed to the Isle of Dogs for my rendezvous with Anders. He greeted me at the station and we walked down to the ground together talking about all the things that had happened since we last met. I told him about my encounter with Helen and he expressed surprise that the separation hadn't brought her round. He was almost apologetic that he'd given me such fruitless advice. I didn't blame him, and I told him as much. He seemed interested in my approach to photography and in getting me some more work.

'I need lots of action Rich. It's for a sport's charity for inner city kids. I know more about the English lower leagues than I do about the Swedish league these days. Watch the number nine. He's tipped for a transfer to a bigger club this summer. If you follow the action it should be quite straightforward but feel free to shoot anything you think captures the sport. Sounds simple. They shoot, they score and we get a lot of positive role models for the kids. Just hope it's not a nil- nil,' he said shrugging his shoulders at me, 'Afterwards, why don't you come round for dinner.'

'Thanks Anders. I'll see how things go,' I said.

'Sure. No pressure.'

Inside the ground I trained my lens on the players as they jogged around the pitch, snapping at the thundering boots as they pounded towards where I crouched with the other photographers beside the goal. After ten minutes the visiting team went ahead. The centre half flicked one into the top left-hand corner. The score remained that way for the next seventy or so minutes. In the stifling frustration of a game that was dying on its feet, every so often I would turn around and take pictures of the crowds. Their sudden bursts of abuse and venom, hope and dashed expectations, solemnity and pessimism told me all I needed to know. They were by far the more fascinating subject. The number nine was photogenic but he either ran too early or too late. He leapt for everything. He launched himself into the penalty box. He did everything but score. Perhaps he could sense that all eyes were being trained on his every

63

movement and this knocked him off his normal game. The manager brought him off to a chorus of abuse from the fans and a young kid from the youth team trotted onto the pitch. Within minutes he had made an impact, latching onto a loose back pass from a defender, darting for the box and smashing the ball into the bottom corner. As the ball ripped the back of the net in the dying embers of the half I caught them all, in a pandemonium of elation, yelling in triumph at their opponents and each other. It was like a reprieve.

7.

The persistent trilling of the phone woke me from a stupendous Pisco hangover and I staggered around the flat trying to find it.

'Am I speaking to Richard?' asked a voice.

'Yes, how can I help you?'

'Ah Richard it's you. So glad you got in touch. You might be able to help me with something.'

'What?'

'You wrote to me more than one week ago. I'm sorry for the delay but I've been at a conference in California. You are the photographer who took the pictures of the crash no?'

'Nikola Petrov?'

'Yes! How is your car?'

'Well, to tell you the truth I've not bothered to do anything about it.'

'Your choice of course.'

'Well, Nikola…'

'Call me Nik. It's less formal.'

'Yes, I was interested in your work on emotional space. You see I'm working on a project that involves…well it involves capturing real emotion….capturing it before anyone realises it's being photographed. It's the reverse of the kind of propaganda we see all the time on people's digital profiles. Am I making sense?'

'Perfectly, we live in a time where people can't be sure if what they're seeing is real or not.'

'Yes, and I wondered if I could do a brief interview with you about that?'

'For a magazine?'

'Potentially, yes. I've got a friend who works for one of the big creative journals. I'm interested in how your work might apply to advertising. I used to produce adverts. I thought we might be able to get together and discuss your ideas.'

'Well, thank you. What in particular are you interested in?'

'I read that you're helping people to re-engineer themselves. How's that going?'

'You have a personal interest? Why don't we meet Richard? Do you have available time on Saturday?'

'Any time you like. Sorry to change the subject but didn't you want to ask me something?'

'It can wait until we meet. See you at the Royal Hotel. At twelve. Is that OK for you?'

'Yes, fine. I'll bring my camera.'

'I'll see you there.'

It was only the second conversation we'd had but he seemed friendlier than I'd expected and very open to meeting a stranger. After the inauspicious start to our first meeting I was fully expecting my email to be ignored. The shock of being woken up had made me feel vulnerable. My poor dehydrated brain was still pounding. I fumbled around the kitchen cupboards for some pills. There were still dozens of bottles of Pisco on the floor; a delivery from Witchetty. They probably couldn't think of anywhere else to send the stuff. So, now after several weeks of struggling on alone I had created an opening, a meeting with someone still new and unfamiliar. I spent the rest of the day checking what was happening in the world. The porn sites had been updated with new girls doing exactly the same things as the previous girls. A bomb had gone off in a hotel killing several people in a suicide attack. More health scares about food. Someone in my timeline had been to an excellent party with some very attractive people. Someone else had gone on a business trip to Holland and got drenched but looked happy beneath an umbrella. A TV celebrity looked much older without her makeup than with it. There had been an influx of good luck messages to a friend who had started her own business. Some immigrants had been found dead in the back of a lorry.

When the day came I got to the Royal Hotel before twelve. Petrov had chosen one of the grand old hotels along the seafront complete with doorman and steps leading up to the Union flags fluttering above a white portico entrance. Inside a tall middle-age man wearing a green jacket awaited me at the reception desk. He glanced at my camera and smiled effusively as I approached him.

'I'm here to interview someone, a Mr Petrov,' I said.

'Of course sir,' he said in a foreign accent 'Please take a seat in the lobby. I'll send someone over to you.'

I took a seat in one of the cracked green Chestertons by the window and tested the camera out on some of the fine decorative plaster work on the ceiling and around the fireplace. I hardly noticed the waitress as she approached me.

'Hello,' she said rather shyly, 'Would you like anything while you are waiting?'

She was a tall and beautifully proportioned young woman, with the broad shoulders of a swimmer and a pointed face. She had an intelligent demeanour.

'Is it OK if I just have some water?'

'Still or sparkling?'

'Just some still water.'

'Would you like a freshly made coffee to go with it?'

'I've just had an espresso thanks.'

'I can make it however you like it. Perhaps half the normal strength. Can I tempt you with a small latte perhaps? And I can give you complimentary biscotti to go with it.'

'OK. Why not? I'll have one.'

She seemed pleased and disappeared into a doorway with my order.

'Not bad was she?' said a voice behind me.

I turned around to see Petrov's grinning face, his nose and beard poking out from behind a high-backed leather chair. I hardly recognized him without his ski-ing goggles.

'Why am I not surprised that you're already here?'

'First or last. It's all in the game my friend. All in the game. Why don't you come round and make yourself comfortable over here?'

I moved around to the chair opposite him and placed my camera down on the table between us. I noticed that he'd brought a tablet with him. I imagined that his online persona was a constant occupation, taking up every spare minute to sustain his followers with bits of comment and opinion. He seemed to be embroiled in something important and was still tapping and swiping the screen as we waited for our drinks. I gathered up my camera and began taking a few test shots of the room. Without looking up he raised a finger as if I myself might be an application that he could pause with a simple stroke or tap.

'Nearly there,' said Petrov, 'I'm in the room with you but not in the room. Haha. Ever get that feeling when someone has checked-out?'

'Very often,' I said.

He tapped away at his virtual keyboard like a thrush tapping at a window with uninterrupted keystrokes as if he were merely transcribing into electronic format the clear blue thoughts of his mind. When he'd finished he folded his tablet into a leather case and smiled, leaning back in his chair.

'So Richard, where shall we begin?'

'It's early stages. I used to work in advertising. Did you see the Fidel adverts? Atlantis? Anyway it doesn't matter. I'm working on a new project. It's freelance stuff. I'm taking some time out from the industry. What I'm going to do is to build up a portfolio of images for an exhibition. I was looking around when I came across your website by chance.'

'I like the way you say you came across my website by chance. That is what we are led to believe. Now, I don't dispute that random landing is a possibility but I'm of the view that nothing we click on is entirely unintended or unplanned. At least not without our own internal compass or that of some outside force guiding us there. It's pre-search; the very anathema of research. It's the idea that we come to the search engine with ideas or intentions that are already formed. Well, be that as it may. You're right. It's my specialism. Whether or not I have something interesting to say....well you can be the judge of that.'

'Perhaps if I take some notes as we chat and then take photos afterwards? Is that OK?'

'Sure, sure. I think your cappuccino is here.'

The waitress returned with the drink and a generously proportioned biscotti. She set it on the table and asked if we needed anything else.

'Nothing for the moment dear,' he said.

I wondered at his easygoing charm. It seemed a long time ago that I'd comforted Matilda at the airshow.

'Do you know her?' I asked.

'Yes, she's one of my students and she helps me with some of my experimental work. She's a perfect example of what I'm researching at the moment.'

'Which is?'

'Paralelismo.'

'What? Paralel-what?'

'ismo. It's Italian. Yes, Paralelismo is a sociological theory which hasn't had too much traction in the past. But here I'm attempting to observe if it's becoming a reality. It's the term we use to describe an increasing awareness that we may be able to lead parallel lives.'

'Can we?'

'Of course, take the girl Dominique who just served us. She is French but living in England. She is studying web technologies rather than continuing in her father's wine export business. She is a waitress today and by night she is an ASMR artist. When you are young you tend to have a greater awareness of your parallel existences. Things are still so fluid. The parallel life of Dominique in France is still only a two hour journey away. She could return to it like that!'

'But once a decision is made you can't go back on it.'

'Can't you?

'Not in my book you can't.'

'Well perhaps your book is only just being written. Ever think of it like that?'

'But you can't re-engineer the past.'

He smiled and shrugged his shoulders as if he thought I'd made a rather innocent observation.

'What you're talking about is leading a double life.' I said.

'No, not really,' he said, 'We are talking about the re-interpretation of the past and the imagination of different futures. Double or triple lives are only part of it. Through use of the internet some people have become acutely aware of the fact that time is a much more flexible concept than they previously thought. In this era of digital access to every corner of people's experience there is more to life than their own seemingly inevitable trajectory. And from this understanding comes a very rational fear that this life is the only one we will ever get. So, why be satisfied with it? We were once more fatalistic, more willing to accept time's constraints. We're not so much like that anymore. We look for ways to step into the parallel lives we might have led… And could still lead if only we have the courage to step into them.'

'You believe this?'

'Travel and technology make it possible.'

'How do you work that one out?'

'Awareness. But even if you look at history you will see examples.'

'Such as?'

'Immigration. Now it's more of a choice.'

'So what kind of work are you doing here? Is it psychology, sociology, digital ethnography?'

'My current project is working with a group of men. These are men who, for various reasons, are interested in unlocking their lives. You should come along and see it for yourself Richard. I'm working with them on their ability to connect with the world, and feel less lonely, which is where they seem to have the most difficulty. This is an age group with a higher than average incidence of suicide. Let me tell you something. Back in Croatia I grew up in a small town. We had everything. Beauty, sea, countryside, sports. It was a paradise for a young man. I had a very close friend who hated the sun and the outside world. He was always plugging into a computer at home. I had to drag him outside. That was until he made the first big leap towards something he really wanted. He fell in love. She was a beautiful girl who walked past his house every day. She was about the same age and she was studying to become a lawyer. I had tried to ask her out on a date a couple of times, but nothing came of it. She was seventeen going on twenty seven, a million light years away. He lost his heart to her and all the poor bastard could do was watch her as she walked to the bus stop every day. I told him he should aim his sights a bit lower. But he didn't listen. He wanted her so much he kidnapped her. He invited her into his house and wouldn't let her go. Devastating for her. Terrifying. When she escaped she went straight to the police. He didn't touch her I believe. She said that all he wanted to do was talk, to find out everything about her. When the police paid a visit to his house they found him hanging from a beam in the garage. Suicide. His family were devastated. The girl was traumatised by the whole ordeal. And I lost a good friend. It's that separation from emotional reality that I'm trying to work on.'

'With smartphones and ipads?'

'It sounds counter-intuitive doesn't it? But it's what

people are doing now. That's my subject.'

I closed my notebook and began gathering up my camera to take a few shots of the crisp and tidy hotel staff in the lobby.

'I hope I've satisfied your interest. Now can I ask you a favour in return?'

I nodded from behind my camera as I tried to work the best angle to take a quick portrait of Dominique.

'I'd like to commission some work from you. For one of my groups.'

I began clicking away as Petrov gesticulated with his large hands. They were fat, labourer's hands rather than the hands of a delicate intellectual.

'First you must come to the university. I'll brief you about it. It's part of an experiment.'

I must have wavered or hesitated for he read my mind immediately.

'Of course, I will pay you,' he said.

I agreed without really weighing it up. I've got nothing to lose. On that note we parted company and agreed to meet again.

I don't really need the extra money at the moment but that wasn't the reason I agreed to go. I had the uneasy feeling that he'd managed to read between the lines of my new life and had spotted something in me that he'd seen before. Something about those theories of parallel reality hit me like a strange drug. As I left the hotel I turned back to see if Petrov might be watching but all I saw was a reflection of myself. It took me by surprise. I looked a little bit older and stranger than I'd expected. And a little bit lost.

8.

I have begun to notice some disturbing changes in myself. The sense of not really being here is gathering pace and there is a certain inevitable logic to it. It feels as though there is a greater distance between myself and everything around me. For instance, just over a week ago a letter written in a neat and sloping hand appeared underneath my front door. Another tenant must have picked it up by mistake and redirected it to me. The blood red frank across the top identified it as something more interesting than a bill. I opened it eagerly. It was from Helen's solicitor requesting that I pick up my things from our former home before they are sent to charity. They had even suggested a beneficiary that I might like to consider. It didn't really register with me at first and I put the letter to one side. I don't feel as though I have any need for the things that I own and certainly don't have any desire to rush back to London to pick them up. This much now seems normal. I made myself a bowl of cereal and sat down in front of the TV to flick through the news channels. Then something unusual happened. When I'd finished eating I walked into the bathroom to brush my teeth. As I checked the mirror I caught a fleeting glimpse of someone pointing a gun into his mouth. It was me. Only it was a vision rather than a genuine reflection. It seemed so real that I looked away and then back at the mirror a couple of times just to see if it had been something to do with the light or an object behind me. I suspect it was probably one of those fabricated images that the mind occasionally conjures up for inexplicable reasons, inserted into the cinema that plays inside our minds. It came and went in an instant. I wasn't sure what to do about it.

What *could* I do about it? So I carried on with what I was doing and got ready to face the day. I didn't want to mention this at first. I'm sure anyone reading this is going to think it's a bit mad and I have to say I'm completely with you but if I'm going to share everything with you then the least I can do is document it. Am I thinking about suicide? I don't think so, but I have begun visualizing it more and more frequently. It has started following me around in different forms. Sometimes when I'm waiting for a bus I'll see a very brief video clip of myself jumping in front of it. On other occasions I've seen myself driving my car at high speed over the cliffs and down onto the sharp white rocks below. The other day I thought I could see someone getting ready to run and jump off the roof of one of the multi-story car parks. It was me. But it's the image of the gun that comes back most frequently although I'm not always pointing it at my mouth. Sometimes I'm pressing it to the side of my head and very occasionally, let's say when I'm reading a book or looking out of the window of a café, I catch myself rubbing my chin with my two forefingers welded together. All of which is slightly laughable and awful at the same time. Am I finally getting to the point where I will kill the old me off? I don't really have any feelings about it. You see it's as if it's not happening to me and I'm looking at it from the point of view of an observer.

All of this brings me to Petrov's invitation. I had to force myself to go. It had been weeks since I'd socialised with people and I felt nervous. I'd put it off for a while but reading up on Petrov's online blog since our last meeting re-ignited my interest. This was the post that I read and I'm copying and pasting some of it here for reference:

What is Paralelismo? By Nikola Petrov

It could be defined as a literary point of view. It's not related to the philosophical concept of Parallelism which is about the separation of actions and reactions. That concept argues that there is no causal relationship between the body flinching in pain at touching a hot saucepan and the mind thinking 'That's hot!'

No, Paralelismo is an awareness that there is always the possibility of more than one life being lived at the same time by the same person. It was first expounded by that famous circle of revolutionary thinkers at the Department of Philosophy in Sienna in the 1970's. It is about thinking of one's self as possessing parallel lives that one could step into like stepping into a film or television drama. It comes from the concept of the multiverse or parallel universes. A person becomes conscious of the fact that had they taken different decisions in the past or if they were to act differently now a parallel reality is open to them. Its parentage is part Surrealism and part Existentialism. The Surreal element comes from the absurd visions and ideas that it's possible to construct from everyday life using tools such as the Internet. The Internet connects people to a whole host of parallel lives that it becomes possible to communicate with and learn from. The existential part is the meaning we give to these parallels and to push them as far as we dare.

To a certain extent the trend in self-improvement is an expression of Parallelismo. People are encouraged by techniques such as visualisation and anchoring to change themselves. The timid public speaker who has to address a wedding party visualizes himself entertaining the crowd and is able to step directly into a parallel reality where he's a confident public speaker. This is a very specific example but in this area of charlatanism and psychology people are attempting to cross over into completely new parallel lives. Even the assumption of different personas on Twitter or in online games, albeit silly or trivial, are nevertheless real expressions of this.

From a literary point of view Paralelismo is the interplay of characters from the past with the present. It involves the characters altering themselves or attempting to alter themselves by entering a new reality. Equally it involves the past actively running parallel with the present and influencing the main characters through a legacy that is still with them.

In this lecture I will set out the new frontiers of Paralelismo art and culture

I called him and arranged to see his next group of Internet guinea pigs. I left the flat after pouring myself a small glass of Pisco to steady the feeling of wanting to be sick. Before I even managed to get out into the street I felt the insistent vibrations of the phone in my shirt pocket like a fitted social pacemaker. It was a message from Matilda. 'How are U? Fancy a drink this eve?' She, more than anyone else, would understand something of Petrov's strange ideas. In my rush to meet him I forgot to text a reply.

I arrived at the university in good time. The first thing I noticed as I walked into Petrov's meeting room were the mannequins. One of them I assumed was the same model I'd caught Petrov with in his car. He'd dressed her for the occasion in a formal black pencil skirt and suit jacket. He'd also put her in high heel boots and given her a wide-brimmed black hat which partially covered her face. The other was a male version, chest exposed to reveal a hard washboard stomach. Petrov was at the front gesticulating about something in front of a flat screen with about a dozen men, seated in front of him, all of whom turned around to face me as I let the door swing shut. I tried to smile and shuffled over to one of the spare seats at the back.

'Everybody. This is Richard. Please make him feel welcome.'

A long-haired man, with a wrinkled brow and grey beard turned around in his seat directly in front of me.

'Glad you could make it,' he said offering a hand and a friendly grin.

'Better late than never,' said a young man with a face that I couldn't decide was friendly or hostile.

I nodded and stared right ahead at Petrov.

'To return to what I was saying,' said Petrov, 'Yes. We sometimes feel as though the screen is where much of our lives are now lived. This is not just an approximation of time. It is a reality. Americans spend an average of twenty three hours per week online. Soon we will have caught up with them. That's more than half a typical working week. Ten years ago it was more like only six or seven hours per week. And it's not the new generation who spend the most time in front of a screen. The age group with the heaviest use of online media are the thirtysomething age group. Exactly the kind of people we have in the room today. So what are we finding out there?'

I waited and watched. Most of the men looked around at each other.

'What's out there? What about women? Aren't they spending the same amount of time in front of the screen looking for similar things?' At this Petrov put a protective arm on the shoulder of his mannequin.

'What about friends? They could all be out there as we speaking. Tapping away in reply to someone or something. Some of them you might never have met face to face.'

'I've got about three hundred. I've met all of them,' said one.

'I keep mine to a nice manageable figure of people I actually keep in touch with,' said the chubby one.

'Well I've just got my first online follower today. How's that for arriving late to the party,' said the grey hair.

At this Petrov paced from one side of the room to the other.

'Five hundred? Ten? One? Does it matter? Why are we sometimes able to communicate so well with a person we never see and yet find it so difficult to communicate with the person sitting next to us in the cafe? It is only because they are completely different ways of connecting. They are not the same thing at all as everyone knows but different. No doubt many of you are very good at chatting with people from distant countries, eloquent at sharing thoughts and experiences with perfect strangers. And yes, I am aware that it's possible to find a connection with each one of them. And yes, I know that it's as real as anything else in this world. It's because most, if not all of them are people like you, doing the same thing as you; finding a reflection of themselves, an antagonist, a sympathizer, a collaborator. But while the interior of your mind is filling up with your collection of peoples what's happening outside? Is it possible to engineer what's happening on the outside world through your interactions online? That is what we are here to try to understand and with your assistance we may discover how this process works. That's if it works at all gentlemen.'

Petrov invited everyone to switch on their laptops and tablets. I drew mine out of my bag and powered it up as discreetly as I could. The grey haired one turned around to speak to me again.

'Are you joining us?' he said.

I naturally felt inclined to nod in agreement.

'Now, let me start by asking you to open your profiles,' said Petrov.

There were some mumbles from the audience about the profiles themselves as each man tried to outdo the other with self-deprecating remarks.

'How you describe yourself online can say a lot about your internal state of mind and is at the same time a beacon, a message in a bottle to the outside world.'

'I disagree,' said a slightly dumpy young man, 'Everyone

lies online. No-one is who they say they are. You've got guys on dating sites pretending they're rich and powerful, and women posting pictures of themselves when they were ten years younger.'

'Ah,' said Petrov bouncing up and down on his toes for a moment, 'This is also true. Very good point. Very good. But if you meet and connect with people in the flesh then you will always be found out.'

'We're just different,' said the grey hair, 'I don't buy that corporate guff about building an online brand. We're not bottles of Coke and none of us could compete with the Diet Coke guy anyway.'

'Speak for yourself my friend,' said a shaven headed one from the front of the group, 'I choose to keep this body in top condition.'

'Is it all just propaganda, gentlemen? Good. Bad. Indifferent. Does it matter? What is the truth about ourselves?' said Petrov, 'Shall we open the dating website we discussed?'

There were a few nods and shuffling in seats from around the group. Petrov walked around to take a look at what his followers had produced for him. He leaned over a few laptops to take a closer look, scrutinizing their pages with a look of intense seriousness on his face. At some pages he raised his eyebrows and at others he turned his mouth downwards like a fish.

'Excellent. I see that you've kept the profiles up to date. What I will need you to do next is to open the survey on the university intranet and click on the link. It will ping the data in there. Profile views, contacts, messages returned. Don't worry. The content of the messages is encrypted and can't be shared. As per the confidentiality agreements we all signed.'

'Now, let me see. That's our starting point. Ground Zero. From here I want you to begin your research. Over the two weeks I want you to conduct a complete survey of the Internet to experiment with your online profile. But first I want to give you a taster to get you started.'

Petrov turned to the flat screen on the far wall and pointed a thin black remote towards it. The screen flickered into life and the words ME appeared in white on a black background.

'Who is Me? How do you define Me? There are three things and only three things that I have found that say everything about you. What you say. How you sound. And lastly, how you look. That's why I've invited a photographer to help us. He's going to take some pictures of you having fun, showing your playful side, your serious side, that kind of thing. Anything until you have the versions of yourself that you would like to present on the profile.'

That was the first introduction to my assignment and it felt as though I had been here before. Heads turned towards me as if they were checking out my credentials. I tried to smile and raised my camera to them briefly to show them it was no joke. I remember thinking, 'let's get on with it, just let me have the money, let's go and I can get back to the flat.'

'So, let's start with Profile Number 1,' said Petrov, 'Now, this is a real profile, absolutely genuine.'

Petrov clicked on the screen and the words ME were replaced with HIM. The words that followed unravelled one by one as if they were being written on the spot by someone behind the scenes. 'Hello! My name is James. I'm not sure what to say but here goes. I work as an actuary for a large insurance company. Sounds a bit boring but it pays the bills. I am tall, average build with brown eyes and go to the gym regularly. I like all kinds of music and sing in a local choir. I also like dining out especially Italian and Thai food, going to the cinema, sports, the outdoors, having a quiet night in front of the TV.'

'Tick lists,' said Petrov, 'How boring!'

The words of the profile kept tumbling out slowly,

'Sadly, my wife died last year but I still like to raise money for the charity that looked after her. I'm looking for a fun and bubbly sort of girl with a good sense of humour who can make me laugh. If that sounds like you then why not drop me a line and tell me a little bit more about yourself.'

'So. What does this profile say exactly? Nothing. It's like many of the profiles out there. It's polite, honest and not particularly pleasing. I can almost guarantee it will generate zero replies. Now look at the picture.'

Petrov clicked his remote and what can only be described as the face of a dishevelled and piggy-eyed monster appeared on the screen. His skin was as white as chalk, his toothy grin so broad and so close to the camera that you could practically see the gum disease. He looked as though he'd just washed himself in the most primitive of supermarket soaps.

'Please don't take a picture of yourself unless you know how to do it. I hope that makes you feel better about your own profile. So, what's his problem? Your profile shouldn't be a window into your soul no matter what anyone says. It should be truthful but not totally transparent. Whatever words you use to describe yourself are the images that will occur in the readers mind. Mentioning what a person does for a living enables other people to include you in their set or exclude you. There are ways of describing things though. Is this man an actuary or is he in the business of predicting the future? If the most interesting thing about you is what you do for a living it had better be good. If you want to drive people away then hint at as much emotional baggage as you can. This poor guy's wife. Whatever happened to her is something he should keep to himself until he gets to know someone better. Now look what this guy turned out several months later.'

Petrov clicked the remote again and this time a series of images of the same man began to play, fading in and out in sequence. He was different alright. As expected, he had tidied up his hair. It was much shorter and must have knocked about five years off him. He'd got some photographs of himself, presumably on holiday, in front of a classical fountain with a blue sky and sunlight giving the impression of a blisteringly hot day. There were also some night-time shots of a very relaxed looking and quite handsome man who you might not object to sitting next to on a plane. Gone were the close-ups and the *au naturel* look of someone who had just woken up.

'So, how did he do that? Who helped him? Did he help himself? We don't know but I have a number of examples like this. From your point of view the next task is to spend some time working on this through your devices. Exploring pathways that contain useful information that you can relate to and then adjusting your profiles according to the ideas that take your interest. I want you to work on these in your own time when you are alone and are not going to be disturbed. I'd like you all to have a new profile up by 30th of the month and then we will monitor the results from that point onwards for at least the next four weeks and compare them with an artificially intelligent profile based on some clever photography of our two mannequins here. This exercise shouldn't take you more than thirty minutes a day. But if you are enjoying yourself you could spend a lot more time. It's up to you. As you are all single men you are more than welcome to follow up on any interest you receive. That part is your own private business and none of your private message can be viewed. At least not by me or anyone at the university.'

'Well I don't know about you', said Steve, 'I don't want to be outdone by some robot.'

I had the distinct impression that I was watching a tightly knit focus group. Petrov appeared to be running it like a marketer, treating each individual as if they were a brand with an intrinsic emotional or spiritual value. I couldn't have run a better introduction to building a brand from the bottom myself. Has he gathered some marketing experience from somewhere in a previous life?

Petrov moved on to his next exercise.

'Now, let's talk about our next subject. This task it a bit trickier but it's important for our research. I said that we would be doing some exercises of practical benefit. This one is going to test your comfort levels, so I have to warn you if you're of a slightly nervous disposition that it might feel a little bit uncomfortable at first. I want you to search for a group online and join it. It can be any kind of group, but it must be something that you can physically join.'

Mark nodded and ran his fingers over his bald head. My initial impression of Mark was of a man who had just emerged from a cave. He had thick arms, a furrowed brow and eyes that seemed to dart nervously all over the room.

'So, some kind of club?'

'If that's what floats your boat. Yes. A cycling club, a support group, a network of entrepreneurs, a gaming society, alcoholics anonymous, weight loss groups. Anything you like. But it must be a group of people who you can meet locally and face to face. It might be a group that you wouldn't usually think of associating with. I don't mean that if you are an environmentalist, you should join a right wing party. Or if you are shy, you should go out dogging. No, something that isn't necessarily your kind of thing will do as long as it attracts your interest. You get my drift. There is a financial bonus for each researcher who completes this part of the exercise over the next few months. Plus, it will be a lot of fun. I hope! Here is a reminder of your instructions on the screen and which I will send to your devices. Any questions?'

'Er, yeah,' said the long-haired hippy one. I think his name is Steve. 'What are we supposed to get out of this? I mean. Why can't you just go to these groups if you want to know about them? What do you need us for?'

'I will explain. This stage is not so much to understand

about the groups but more about people. And men in particular. What kind of stresses and strains does it exert on a man to leave his home and attempt to integrate into a new group. How does it affect his health, his wellbeing? What are the challenges and difficulties? This is much more interesting than the group itself. If you want to choose your group carefully then be my guest. If you can make it realistic and true to life then great. Are we OK?'

There was nodding from the men around the room.

'Copy that Professor,' said Mark, 'You want to see what we have to go through not to be alone.'

'That's a good way of putting it. Now for a quick exercise that may help you before you set out on this journey. Are we all ready? Could everyone stand up please?'

Petrov skirted around the floor getting everyone into position. Each man faced his partner at arm's length and looked as though they were about to greet an unknown colleague at an ice-breaker, displaying a mixture of readiness and embarrassment. I seized the chance to document some of this with my camera as I suspect Petrov had intended me to. The first exercise was simple. Each man had to stand, silently in front of his partner and play a game of mental rehearsal. 'Let your arms fall by your sides, relax, breathe from your stomach,' Petrov kept saying, 'Think of at least three very positive things about yourself that make you who you are, things that you are proud to be. Don't say them. Just think them and keep eye contact with the person in front of you. Always keep the eye contact. This is very important. Now think of three things about the person standing in front of you. Three things. Positive things. Things that you would be happy to say to that person if you knew them already. Ok now practice this when you meet people. Notice what's good about them. Now you can introduce yourselves to each other.'

I began to feel as though I was stuck in a training programme for a department store. The men had been standing around like silent mannequins for the most part, working on their inner thoughts. Suddenly the room was bursting with energy and chatter. Men were laughing, talking to one another like friends. Petrov was rehearsing something, but it wasn't clear to me just what he was trying to achieve. He walked around placing a hand on a shoulder here or adjusting someone's body there.

'Fantastic. Excellent. Now, I want you to practise the state you were in just now when you go out and about in your daily lives. But please don't stare at people for five minutes before you say hello.'

There was laughter from around the room and for the first time in months I found myself laughing aloud. Petrov approached me for a quiet word.

'So, Richard, what do you think?'

'It's a bit strange but then who am I to judge?' I replied.

'It is strange isn't it? Everything is becoming that little bit stranger don't you think? Now, are you ready for our assignment?' asked Petrov.

'How many hours is this going to take?'

'I'll pay you. Don't worry. All will be well. It shouldn't be more than a couple of hours. What I want you to do is get the raw essence. Flatter them a little but capture them as the men they are capable of being. The men who stand in parallel to themselves.'

9.

It was a bigger undertaking than I'd expected. That much became clear and no amount of money or creative nous could make this gang of celibates appear attractive. We all left the hotel together; Petrov, Mark, James, Steve, Neil and the others and emerged onto the seafront on a stupendously sunny afternoon. The light was perfect. The flowers hanging from the hotel entrance had blossomed into rich purples, whites and reds. The sky and the sea were like strips of blue cloth laid out on a table. Petrov put on his yellow sun goggles and marched off in the direction of the pier. The rest followed him, occasionally turning around to check that I was still in tow. I suspect that some of them were wondering when they'd have to pose for the camera; to be self-conscious or not to be self-conscious. We bobbed and weaved through stalled traffic to get to the pier entrance where Petrov gathered his group around him.

'Let's just have some fun, OK. Do whatever comes into your mind,' he announced.

It wasn't easy at first. I could tell the men were anxious and unused to the presence of the camera. They stuck together using the sea as the backdrop, with arms round each other like a gang of stags. Petrov tried to show them the way by jumping up onto an old-fashioned carousel, looking out towards the horizon on a white horse like Napoleon. I got that one all too well, but the problem was that the others tried to copy him. It descended into a farcical routine of taking pictures of one silly looking male after another with none of the natural warmth I was looking for. I was grateful when they got hungry and were enticed by the smell of vinegar and the deep fat fryers. At last I was able to get some natural shots of men doing what truly makes them happy: eating. I think it was Steve who first attracted some attention. In his case it was a seagull. She may have been female. In any case she was an enterprising thief who crept up behind Steve's shoulder, whipping the bag of chips from his hand and carrying them off to a rock nearby. He was utterly amazed by what had happened. I got that one on camera. *The scavenger seizing its chance.* Laughter rolled over the group like an incoming tidal wave. The shots got better. I got one of Mark, the ex-royal marine, looking pensively at the horizon which I think offered him something different, a contrast to his brash energy.

Soon Petrov was leading us down to the theme park at the pier's end and the old rides painted in red, blue and gold. I think it was Steve, the old hippie, who suggested the roller coaster. Everyone else followed his lead, jumping on board the carriages, faltering as they tried to climb the steps, halting one of the more diminutive members of the group for failing to meet the height restriction. He posed next to it for my benefit. Mark tried to organise a Mexican wave, which broke down every time it fell upon Steve's uncomprehending shoulders. I followed all this from the side-lines, standing beside the white picket fence guarding the entrance until they were off. They climbed the first steep incline and disappeared over the brow of the track at high speed. That was the last I saw of them until they turned up at the exit, still laughing and ribbing each other. James affected 'jelly legs' as he climbed out of the carriage. Mark and Tim did mid-air high-fives. Only Neil looked unimpressed, rolling his eyes at me and shuffling off to find another ride. Soon, I was following them to the Cage of Death, a ride where they were strapped inside a metal cage and spun around from a great height like being strapped to the sails of a windmill. I got some great before and after shots of James who had been hiding in the background for most of the day.

And so it went on, me trailing them as they scampered from one ride to the next; losing themselves in their horseplay. It wasn't a complete waste of my time. I might be able to use some of the shots for my collection and there are at least a couple for each of the men. Some capture a mood or a moment where they are clearly unaware of themselves. Some of the shots could easily fill out a billboard. Steve and the seagull; a friend to nature, a man with a sense of humour, an unselfish man, a man you could trust.

When it was over they all wanted a drink and we made for a beer garden nearby. Petrov bought in a round and I could see how he held their trust. He filled me in on some of them. Mark was a former captain who had served in Afghanistan and Steve had run some kind of New Age shop which had closed down after his wife had left him. Neil gave very little away but Petrov recommended him for advice on mortgages. They were worlds apart but joined by their disenchantment with the world. A couple of women sat down at a table next to us and he immediately engaged them in conversation. I thought he did this unknowingly and on reflection I wonder if he was not just trying to obtain another window into another soul. He was never off duty.

Steve beckoned me to sit down with him.

'Come on man. Why don't you put the camera down and have a drink with us,' he said.

I slumped next to him, tired and exhausted.

'I bet you think we're crazy don't you?' he asked.

'I'm just here to do a job,' I said.

'Yeah,' said Mark, 'He definitely thinks we're crazy.

'Do you get a lot of this kind of work?' asked Steve.

'Far from it. Most people take pictures of themselves these days.' I said.

'Yeah I don't really dig that,' said Steve, 'I never cared about how I looked and now this guy is trying to get me to think about my style. I don't have a style. I mean, the last time I bought any clothes was from the Save the Planet charity shop. Is there a style for that?'

'Yeah. Confused,' added Mark, 'That's not what he's saying. You've got to get to the real you. The style you already have. Then you live it, breathe it. Tidy it up. Make it appealing. That's what he's saying.'

'Maybe,' said Steve. 'I don't like the way relationships work anymore. It was more romantic before the Internet. Eyes meeting over dinner. It was slower. There was more of a build up.'

'Nice,' said Mark, 'But there isn't time for all of that now. People just don't meet each other like that when they live on their own. Young people do but not us. You're either locked down in a marriage situation or locked out. That's why everyone works long hours.'

'Speak for yourself,' said Neil, 'We socialise with women at the office all the time.'

'Yeah, but how many do you count on as friends?' asked Mark.

'Ok, I take your point,' answered Neil.

'See,' Mark went on, 'All we do is head back to our flats on our own or hang out with other men. This experiment is finally giving me some ideas. It's about taking on the bad stuff. It's about spreading out, getting to know more people. You can't get anywhere without people.'

Steve shrugged his shoulders and said, 'It's it all rather sad? Looking for love isn't like ordering a pizza. You can't just order it online and it'll turn up on your doorstep.'

'Why not? Have you actually used the Internet recently because I can't believe you just said that.'

'So, what's your style Mark?' asked Neil.

'I don't have one,' said Mark, 'That's the problem. I was in Afghanistan for two years. I got wiped clean. Creeping around looking for Taliban concentrates the mind on the basics. How do I avoid getting my legs blown off tomorrow? Nothing else matters. This guy is finally making me think about who I am again.'

I noticed that Petrov had moved closer to us.

'I hope you enjoyed it today. It was good. All good,' he began, 'But what we are really missing is some night time shots. Get ready for an evening out next week. Smartest clothes gentlemen. In fact, I want you to look like gentlemen. I have a challenge for you that I think you'll enjoy.'

'What's that?' asked one of the men.

'Ah, that's a surprise. A couple of things you need to do on the night. The first is to arrive here at ten thirty sharp. The other is to dress well and remember to be sober. I mean it. No drinking at all. Goodbye gentlemen. I'll see you on the other side.'

With that he took off down the seafront and strutted past the bronze statue of a racing horse, past the tulip gardens and bandstand until I could no longer distinguish his tall, striding figure from the milling crowds around him. I turned back to the group.

'Well,' I began, 'You heard what he said. I guess I'll see you all here next week.'

They stood behind me like a herd of bullocks in a field, looking around as if they weren't sure what to do next.

'When do we get the pictures?' asked Neil, 'I could do with putting them up as soon as possible.'

'I'm afraid I know no more that you do. Soon I suppose,' I replied.

I said my farewells and headed back into the city. I remembered Matilda's text. It was still early evening and as good as any time to meet. I sent a reply without expecting her to get back to me. She didn't hesitate. The message that arrowed its way back and buzzed in my shirt pocket read 'Meet you at the Punch and Judy Bar at 7.30 x'.

I arrived before her. The bar was already quite full. I saw a woman standing on the fringes of a group of men in suits. She looked directly at me and our eyes met for a second before she looked away and returned to her group. Before meeting Petrov it wouldn't have occurred to me that this was anything more than a woman's boredom with her immediate company. Now, I began to speculate that her body language might be a transmitter for making new connections, a beacon of social capital. It irritates me to think that he has already filtered my perceptions so easily that even his way of expressing himself has begun to hold court in my mind. I ordered a drink and waited for Matilda. Yes, Matilda. What has happened to us? Before, it was just nice to know a friendly face in the city but now I wonder if she too might be some lonely mannequin in an android world. Was that what my ex Helen had been? Had she checked out the available males on offer and opted for a new one based on superior specifications? I could feel the influence of Petrov again and his lecture on the multiplicity of life experiences in the digital world. I was grateful when Matilda finally showed up.

'Hi, how are you? What's up? You look a bit stressed,' she said.

'Nothing a glass of Pisco wouldn't cure,' I said.

'Tell me about it. I had a shit day at work. I really need a large one.'

'Listen, sorry I couldn't make it to the party.'

'Yeah,' she sighed, 'You'd have really liked it. Quite a mix of interesting people. I didn't know half of them. There were a couple of artists there. They were from Spain I think, and we got talking with them for most of the night. I hope you don't mind but I recommended they check you out online.'

'No, not all. Sounds like I missed out twice over. Unfortunately, I was on an assignment in London.'

'Any good?'

Something odd is happening to my conversations with people. I have started to notice what I am going to say before saying it. It's as if I can predict what my next line will be, as if it's already written down on a script somewhere.

91

'Yes. Some great pictures. Monkey faces in a crowd.'

'Monkey faces? Were you at the zoo or something?'

'A football stadium. Same thing.'

'Can I see? I'd love to help. Why don't you let me help you to organise something? You know, I could be your publicity machine. I'd be happy to start finding a gallery for you. Listen, I know someone from the party the other night who's just done an exhibition at the city library. It'd be so cool if you could get your work there. You'd really like it. They've got a really big white space for installations.'

'Well….' I said knowing full well that this was what I was meant to say.

'Oh, go on. It would be fun to get involved in promotions.'

'Ok, as long as it's not going to put you out.'

'It's not going to. Don't worry.'

We talked on into the night. Well, Matilda talked and I mainly listened. She talked about her boss, her friends, the airshow accident, religious belief, gay and lesbian bars, her experiences with arty types at college and I chipped in stories about hair raising creative briefs on the edge of waterfalls and wild tequila nights in Mexico. I even mentioned Petrov and his Flying Circus.

'Oh, he's a professor of some kind isn't he,' she said, 'He's quite clever. I think I'm following him.'

'He's probably following you,' I said.

'Do you think you could help me to get a job in London, in your industry?' she asked out of the blue.

Matilda's cheeks flushed red. I couldn't be sure, couldn't be really certain that what I was about to say wasn't going to kill those first feelings of attraction we seemed to have for one another and bind us into a transactional relationship. Either way offered compromise. I answered according to the script which was to say that I was happy to recommend her to some colleagues in the business and in doing so abandoned any hopes I had of inviting her back to my place.

Nature's trick is to convince the subject that the mechanical actions and reactions of love are in some way spontaneous and profound and have no ulterior motives. I continued as if none of this mattered and even though I thought I could glimpse an image of myself destroying my life all over again, we carried on laughing late into the night.

10.

Internet Browsing History for 30th July

00.06 - Twitter - Nikola Petrov
00.09 - Twitter - Nikola Petrov's followers
00.36 - Twitter - MatildaTheUnready
00.46 - Twitter - MatildaTheUnready's followers
00.57- Twitter - MatildaTheUnready's favourites

We were both dead drunk by the end. I caught a taxi with her and dropped her home, watched her skip down the path leading to the front door of her parent's house, waited until she had closed the door behind her then asked the driver to take me home. The driver grinned at me from the rear view mirror. I could barely keep both feet on the ground when it was time for me to get out of the cab. If I could have safely rolled out of my seat onto the pavement and fallen asleep I would have done. Instead I made myself climb the stairs up to the apartment, gripping the banister tightly like a rope. I can't have been making much headway because before long I felt a shove to my shoulder and a guy with a shaven head and a leather coat burst past me muttering something in a foreign tongue

I was slow to react. I watched him disappear round the corner to climb the next flight of stairs. I hadn't heard him coming. I stopped for a moment and reached for my arm, feeling some pain where he had pushed me against the banister. As I neared the landing I heard a door open and the whisper of a female voice and the sound of footsteps, of shoes on tiled floor. I tried not to look, wary of another confrontation only to catch a glimpse of another man. He looked like Mark. The man rushed past me. I turned to look behind me but he was gone. At the top of the stairs I noticed that my neighbour's door was slightly ajar. A young woman with long, curly black hair poked her head around the door, smiled at me and then slammed it shut. It was a strange ending to an unusual day. I burst into my flat after fumbling with the door handle and made straight for bed. Judging by the state of the flat in the morning, the sink full of opened jars, plates and knives I'd also made a few trips to the kitchen during the night.

The next day I registered on the website that Petrov had recommended to his students. I wanted to find out what he was up to and with the afternoon to kill I settled down in front of my laptop. I assigned myself an identity, *cyberneticgreeneyes* in honour of the many lonely hearts I found online; *bootygirl81*, *ladygreyeyes*, *sirenheart90*. The website insisted that I upload a photograph before continuing and so I turned the camera lens on myself, using a timed switch to give myself a fighting chance. In the first set of pictures I looked impassive and emaciated. I smiled for the next few. These were not much better. The smiles looked fixed and bleached of colour and vigour. For Christ's sake. I can't even take a good picture of myself. Do I need someone to do it for me? Instead I chose something from my stock of images from the archives, a portrait of the obscure French photographer Roman Meunier. He'd been dead since 1991 so I trusted he wouldn't mind.

I filled in the rest of the online form, stripping down my personality into representative ideas and themes, keeping the career stuff to a bare minimum. I wasn't careless about this. Like an advert I wanted to appeal to the right kind of consumer who would quickly be able to switch on or off according to what was on offer. I didn't think too much about what I might want. Nor did I write more than a few words in 'similar interests' to hook anyone following me. How could I after witnessing Petrov's little lecture? Once I was done I had a brief look at the number of females registered as living in this city and then the number of males. There was a considerable imbalance. What happens to the product when it doesn't match up to the ad?

I read through several pages of women. Clicking through the profiles was like skimming through a bookshelf. Isn't it the title of the book or the art on the cover that tempts you to pick it up? *ladygreyeyes* was the first to grab my attention. She certainly looked like the kind of woman I liked. Her photos depicted a sleek figure in long boots, chic dresses, set against romantic European locations (I think I spotted Capri in the background) and with immaculately toned arms, legs and a chiselled nose and chin. So far so good. What did she like?

'I enjoy riding, skiing, scuba diving, travelling and experiencing new cultures, fast cars, cookery, fine wines, rock concerts, body painting.'

And her personality?

'Easygoing, vibrant, witty, controversial and characterful, warm and generous to my friends…'

And her ideal man?

'Alpha male who knows what he wants and is successful in his field but who is also warm, passionate and kind.'

No. I couldn't see it myself. Any man who attached himself to her would need to be rich, powerful and able to weather a storm of hyperactivity.

Next up was *belleamour*. She seemed a little more down to earth; educated, confident, steady.

Her profile poured scorn on any false male expectations:

'Having shopped around at the man market only to take home damaged goods I thought it only fair to give you an idea of what's NOT on my shopping list. The following men need not apply.

a) If you can't see your toes from a standing position

b) If you've never travelled.

c) If you think that a conversation is a contest of opinion

d) If you don't go out at least four nights a week.

e) If you don't read novels

f) If you've ever lacked the courage to change your job, career, relationship.

No, to d) then, but despite feeling relieved that I'd met most of the criteria I wasn't quite sure where she was going with the damaged goods remark. I mean aren't we all? Hadn't she read Larkin's *This be the Verse*? *They fuck you up your mum and dad, they may not mean to, but they do.*

Someone else had chosen to lead with the negative approach; *KarmaPussy4500*. I had to hand it to her. Her '10 reasons not to respond to my profile' were refreshing to say the least. *Not good in the mornings. Hopeless at cooking. Won't be much good at pretending to like sports. Opinionated.* Her picture was a close up of a classic beauty with long blonde locks, a perfectly symmetrical pair of eyes, plucked eyebrows and a sleek aquiline nose. We used this reverse engineering for certain elite products and no amount of negativity would stop consumers lapping it up. I wonder how Petrov's stock of subjects are getting on? Does he believe that they could still make a connection with these beings with more strings attached than a turtle caught in a deep sea fishing net. This truly would be a parallel shift in their current lives. I changed the search parameters, increasing the age range to forty, broadened the selection criteria to any shape or size. They were far more curvy, middle-aged, mumsy looking, with a history of relationships and disappointed expectations. Was that really what James and the others were hoping to achieve to escape from their isolation? Did Petrov believe that by trawling through the Internet the men might just catch a mermaid in their nets? In the midst of this miasma of dampened hopes I spotted a name that caught my eye; *ElectrikTanya*. Her profile picture depicted a dog rather than a woman's face with another picture of an upper thigh caressed by stockings and a garter. Before I could uncover any more about her there was a knock at the door.

When I opened it there was a young woman standing outside in skinny jeans and bright red, plastic shoes with a latte in one hand and a handbag attached to her arm. She smiled and shrugged apologetically,

'Sorry I wake you. I have no key,' she said. She knocked on her door again, waited for a minute, rummaged in her handbag, looked at her phone and began tapping a message.

'Did you knock?' I said.

She looked up at me and shook her head.

'No, she must be out. I'll wait.'

'Ok, if you want to wait here that's fine. I can make you a drink, a coffee or something?'

'Thanks I already have one. I wait,' she replied.

I closed the door and returned to my laptop.

She wasn't the girl from the night before. I felt sure of it. I wonder if Mark has already built up a connection with someone? Did he precipitate the arrival of the man who'd muscled me aside on the staircase only moments before? A jealous boyfriend? I don't remember any shouting or scuffling. In the state I was in I probably wouldn't have noticed anyway.

Back at my keyboard I'd received a message.

ElecktricTanya winked at you

I clicked on her profile. She claimed to like Chekhov and documentary films. She gave her profession as a curator and described herself as 'a confirmed adrenalin addict'. Her taste in music ranged from Edith Piaf to ABBA and if that wasn't enough to convince me of her near certain insanity or doubt the authenticity of her profile I saw that her interests also included 'blogging and nature photography.' Despite this she was the only person to wink at me so far and so I thought I'd follow the script and send her a message. What else was there to do?

A voice from outside the flat told me that something was finally happening for the stranded girl. It was a vivacious tone, an older woman's voice, speaking as if she had discovered a long lost relative. There seemed to be a lot of excited laughter, so I went to the door to listen. I could hear her clucking away and jangling a set of keys as she talked endlessly in a foreign language. Once the two women were inside the flat I could hear muffled voices and the sound of doors, perhaps wardrobes being opened and closed. I went back to the images I'd taken yesterday and began working through them, selecting and cropping, enhancing and framing them. Progress was slow, and I was often distracted by the sound of the television next door, the volume of which had been turned right up.

11.

It gets weirder. It's been over a week since I last posted but I must relay the events of last night. Petrov's research continues. I had to follow him and headed down to the rendezvous he'd agreed with his subjects the last time we met. They were all there, shuffling around in open-neck shirts and smart jackets, waiting for the errant prophet to arrive but he was evidently running late. I saw Mark and Steve first, and waved at them. Mark nodded in my direction, but he was talking to someone on his phone. Neil was standing near the road glaring at passing traffic. He looked as though he'd come straight from the office. I've not had much of a chance to get to know him so far, so I hung back to talk to him.

'So, you turned up,' I said.

He smiled briefly.

'Do you have any idea what he's got lined up tonight?' I asked.

'Nope, and neither does he if last week was anything to go by,' he replied.

'Soon I'll be able to release the photos we took the other week.'

'I'd prefer not to have to go through the rigmarole of using them but needs must I suppose.'

'How'd you get to know Nik?'

'I blog about the local property market and I found him through his own blog. He's a semi-amusing restaurant critic outside of his academic persona. Plus, he promoted my blog to his followers. Have you seen it?'

He began to show me his phone.

'I've seen it,' I said, 'But apart from that?'

'Apart from that? I don't feel as though enough is happening in my life. Don't you find that? It's very demanding but at the same time it lacks variety. This is an interesting psychological diversion and we get paid for it.'

A black BMW pulled up beside us and the window on the passenger side began to descend to reveal a blonde girl in a pink dress. She waved at us invitingly. Petrov's head lurched into view as he leaned across her to speak to us.

'Hello! How are you? Would you mind telling the others that I've arranged cars to pick them up? Why don't you and Neil jump into mine.'

I noticed a fleet of three black cabs with darkened windows pulling up behind Petrov. Neil trotted over to the others to relay his instructions while I jumped in next to him.

'Stella this is Richard. Richard this is Stella,' he said as I buckled myself in.

She extended her hand to me. I shook hands and noticed how firm her grip was.

'Pleasure,' I said.

'Stella's going to tag along this evening,' said Petrov.

Neil climbed in and was greeted with a shy smile from Stella.

'Hi,' he said without making much eye contact. The confidence of only a few minutes before had slipped away. Petrov nodded at me briefly and we drove on into the night, cruising through the city centre streets and gliding past the bright, loud revellers who got so close to the car they might have easily fallen under it.

We pulled up outside one of the busiest clubs in the city; the *Vida Loca*. Petrov knows people. As soon as he had pulled up he handed the car keys to a man in a tuxedo who obediently waited for us all to disembark before climbing into the driver's seat and steering the car away. I turned around to see Petrov ushering the men from the taxis as they pulled up behind us, gesturing for them to enter through a side entrance usually reserved for VIPs. People in the queue leaned over to catch a glimpse of us. I took a few shots of the guys and the beautiful Stella. I lingered outside for a few more minutes, taking shots of the waiting punters before I followed the men through the side door. By then I had lost them and found myself surrounded by a heaving mass of people clustered around tables and staircases. Transfixed by the rhythm of the music I climbed the stairs to a balcony overlooking the dancefloor watching groups of people absorbed by the music. The men were nowhere to be seen. It was then that I felt a tap on my shoulder.

'I need to talk to you,' yelled a voice and I sensed who it was before I'd even turned around. Of course, it had to be Petrov. He beckoned me to follow him into one of the private bars on the upper floors where 'it would be quieter.' I followed him up the stairs as I imagined all his followers did, wondering what he was up to next. He bounded up those stairs and I followed him, becoming increasingly breathless until we arrived at the entrance to a rooftop terrace. It was like a garden, filled with fluorescent pink and turquoise Chinese lanterns leading to a fountain filled with red and white carp. We walked along the paving stones in silence until Petrov found a spot overlooking the city at night. He stared out to sea, inhaling the night air in deep, controlled breaths.

'Peace at last. It feels so much better up here don't you think? Stella likes nightclubs but in all honesty I can't bear them.'

'That doesn't sound like you,' I said.

'Doesn't it?' said Petrov, 'I would much prefer to be with smaller groups of people. There are too many. Too many. It makes me feel claustrophobic.'

'Stella seems like a nice girl.'

'She is. You like her eh? How did you like the photos you took of the men?'

'I did my best to make them appear as relaxed as

possible. Can I ask you something? Don't you think adding Stella changes things? If I take some pictures tonight with her around won't it give a false impression?'

'And you say you used to work in advertising?'

'It's not like any campaign I've ever worked on. This is totally different.'

'No, but is it really? Advertising is the devil's work. All the psychological research showed you that you could influence people if you did it indirectly, subliminally. It was advertising that suggested to men that they needed to have things and own things in order to be worth something. You may have had a hand in this too.'

'Up to a point but nobody has to buy the stuff.'

'Ah, the get out clause. You are being disingenuous with me I think. But now we have perhaps the greatest advertising window in history; the Internet. The only difference is whether these men can still navigate it to fulfil their potential or whether they need interventions on how to do it. Advertising is not just for companies. Everyone is doing it. Nothing is off limits. It's a distraction from reality. But I'm not trying to sell these guys. If they choose to they can find hundreds of different ways to reconnect with the world. All I am doing is testing out a certain number of controlled pathways for their brains to follow including the way they advertise themselves. We will then see which ones they take. And why. That is if they take them at all. Take away the belief that they have to be good consumers, good workers, buy the right things, go to the right places in order to be valued and perhaps they can get back to controlling their own reality.'

'I'm sorry,' I said, 'But how do you know they're not learning how to manipulate their perception of reality? What if the way they advertise themselves is not something they can live up to?'

'Oh, I can't predict that. No-one can.'

There was an uncomfortable period of silence.

'Perhaps I'd better go back,' I said.

'No, not yet. Stay. Can I see the photographs?'

I handed over my phone. He flicked through a couple, occasionally turning the camera at an angle to get a better appreciation of the image he was looking at. He nodded and handed the phone back to me.

'What do you think?' I asked.

'They need to have the final say on which, if any of the images they use, but this gives them a bit more choice now. Can you send them over to me? In fact, why don't you come over to my flat so that we can download them directly? I can pay you at the same time.'

I was still curious to know what this man's life was really like and a glimpse of his home afforded unimagined possibilities.

'And how are you Richard? Is everything OK?' he asked.

'I'm surviving.'

'And work?'

'Not much, I've got a trip to Manchester for a freelance job next week.'

'And your personal life?'

'OK, yeah. Everything's OK.'

'Have you embraced your new life yet? Or is it still on the horizon?'

'I'm not sure. I logged onto the dating website you lot use and got winked at. She's not one of your stooges is she?'

'No. Not at all. How could it be? Meet her and you'll see.'

'Can I ask you a question of a personal nature? I hope you don't mind. I saw you with someone completely different at the airshow. Another woman.'

'Oh yes,' said Petrov, 'So you did. Well it's no secret. Stella knows about Vivienne and Vivienne knows about Stella. We are friends. Well, what did you expect? I only have so many hours in the day. Occasionally I meet a new woman who's really very interesting and we have a fling.

104

This time I met two. But Stella and Vivienne have no need of a serious relationship at the moment and so we work it out. I would be a hypocrite to object and so we never talk about that. Have you got time to come back to my place and I'll show you how the research is progressing? Tonight is just a bit of fun to see if they have applied any of the exercises on non-verbal communication. I'd be grateful if you could take a few more photos before we go and then when you're ready let's pick up Stella and say goodbye to our friends. Shall we?'

Over an hour later we were in Petrov's car, Stella in the seat next to her friend, me in the back and heading over to his flat.

'I don't want to keep you up,' I said.

'No problem. I have to go home to get some sleep now,' Stella answered.

'You pose like a professional. Were you a model by any chance?' I asked.

'Yes, I was professional model in Poland. And you? You're not new to photography?'

'No, but it's a long story.'

We dropped Stella off somewhere on the far side of town. I watched Petrov escort her up a flight of steps leading up to the front door of a peeling but still genteel three-storey town house. When he'd kissed her goodbye and returned to the car Petrov turned to me before we set off.

'You saw the house no? Beautiful. She owns it. It's hers. Just her and her little son Pavel. She's done so well from modelling and escorting that she can afford to do a few part-time jobs here and there. That's where I met her. Working as a waitress in a café by the sea. She has a degree in modern languages from the university Wroclawski.'

'She seems very nice,' I said.

'So, you still like her eh?' said Petrov.

'She's also very quiet. Not my type but fine'

We crept slowly past the drunks and revellers as they

spilled out into the city centre. Petrov took a diversion along the sea front to avoid them, taking in the hotel lobbies with their names in lights, the Grand, the Palace, glittering in the dark. When we arrived, it was at a purpose-built new complex surrounding a marina. It wasn't quite finished. Apart from a few cranes that still occupied the eastern fringes of the site most of it was lived in. At least I assumed people lived there. Petrov drove up to the entrance of one of the blocks and pulled out a remote control. A corrugated metal door rolled upwards to allow us to descend into the basement car park below. He parked up between a Lotus and a Mercedes and somewhat overshadowed by the high life he seemed to be living on a lecturer's wage, we made our way to the stairwell and climbed up two flights of stairs to get to his front door.

'This is not university accommodation as you know it eh?' began Petrov, 'Quite often these flats are rented to the weekenders; yacht owners and their so-called friends. It affords me some comfort, it's private and it has the most modern technological developments in living space. Low lights! TV!'

As he voiced his instructions the lamps in the corners of the lounge flickered dimly and a large flat screen TV began came to life, displaying one of the twenty-four hour news channels. The interior was not what I'd expected. It was technological in appearance rather than homely. Flat screen TVs were mounted on several walls like giant *tabula rasa* for recording his projected thoughts.

'Make yourself at home,' he said, 'Would you like a drink?'

He invited me to sit in one of the black sofas surrounded by white curtains and walls. A picture of a vase of lilies painted on a black background hung from the walls. Every unit, every vase, every rug was either black or white; a lounge decorated in binary code. That's not to say that I didn't like it. I drank it all in. It wasn't exactly like walking into a home decorated by a zebra. Far from it. The contrasts were subtler than that and appeared to be carefully orchestrated.

'You like?' he shouted from the kitchen.

'What's not to like?' I replied.

'Imagine a room with all the baggage from the past stripped out. That's how I see it.'

Petrov returned to the lounge with two glasses of whiskey on ice. He handed me a drink and then fell back into a wrinkled leather chair.

'What do you think of the guys?' he asked.

'They were more confident than the first time I met them. More certain. Is that the word I'm looking for? Sure of themselves perhaps. But I'm not surprised by the kind of men who volunteer for these things. Lonely. Depressed.'

'You think so? Interesting. That happens to be the subject under study.'

'What was tonight about anyway?'

'Confident communication in an uncertain social environment. The means to establish a way of overcoming internal struggles and contradictions to live life well. And it was a bit of fun to keep them happy. But the outcome is uncertain. These men are not lonely or in pain as a result of anything we are doing. That is an ever-changing emotional state. But they have come forward because they want to be able to re-calibrate their lives. They were lonely before.'

'What about Mark,' I said, 'He seems to think this is his ticket to finding a woman like Stella?'

'Sure. Why not?' said Petrov, 'Mark is an example of what I'm talking about. The ongoing escape attempt from the reality prison. He told me that he started seeing escorts when he came back from Afghanistan. Did you know that he went from being one of the most committed to the war to being completely against it? It completely cut through his sense of reality. The army has effectively ostracised him. He's stranded. Escorts are the kind of sympathetic people who will listen to him.'

'But it's not really listening is it? They're paid to do that.'

'How do we know? What's real is often only a simulation. And what's a simulation can seem real. Who are you and I to be able to tell the difference?'

'What about James? Do you really think he could ever become socially adept? The guy's borderline autistic.'

'Unlike you I do believe. I've seen it,' he said and logged in to the flat screens situated around the house. Then he motioned for me to look at the one above the fireplace.

'Here,' he said pointing to a picture of a bare-chested man in trunks standing on a sandy beach. The man was attempting to pose like a body builder drawing ironic attention to the lack of any muscle on his sinewy body, 'This was a great guy. Oh, a fantastic guy. He was one of the top airline pilots for his company. A very precise and reliable guy. He was a perfectionist, one of those people who puts his life into a very specific order. It made him the perfect pilot. He needed very little sleep. He never drank very much. Never got tired. When I met him he had a very intense stare. His eyes seemed to be open just that fraction too much. Do you see? Slightly too wide-eyed if you understand me. Quite unsettling but not deliberate. One day he woke up and couldn't get on another plane. He convinced himself that the very next flight he took control of would lead to a disaster. He was totally convinced that he couldn't trust himself anymore. He thought he would endanger the lives of his passengers. There were some clues in his background. His mother had died a couple of years before. He'd had a few nice girlfriends but never settled down. He earned enough money to live an independent life. After something like ten years of flying he ran into a wall. Now look at him.'

Petrov flicked to a second photograph. It showed a scruffy looking, chubby figure with long wavy hair peering over a pair of Ray bans perched on the end of his nose. A petite young woman, smiling sweetly into the camera, hugged his ample torso.

'Is this the same man?' I asked.

'Yes, look at the scar across his forehead. It's the same no?' Petrov zoomed in on both images to allow me to compare.

I checked. It was identical.

'What's he doing now?'

'He's a chef. Hence the weight. Much happier in this life than his other one. The pretty young thing in the photo is his wife. An Albanian waitress. Loves him to distraction I'm sure. He emailed me this following one of my previous projects. This is just one of many case studies.'

'If you start living another life aren't you throwing away the one you've lived? Betraying who you really are? Or worse, it's actually pretending to betray who you are because who you are never changes. Ok, you can change profession and all that but we're born a certain way. Our family, our genes. All that weight of history and upbringing on your shoulders can't just be moved to one side. It's not like uninstalling a software programme and re-installing a new one. Without meeting him I couldn't tell you if this guy wouldn't be better if he'd just taken a long break before getting back up in the air again.'

'I wonder why you of all people are resistant to this idea Rich?' asked Petrov.

'Why?'

'Are you not in fact stepping into a parallel life of your own? Moving city. Leaving behind your girlfriend. Changing profession. I thought you of all people would understand.'

'No, it's not like that with me. I feel like I'm being changed from without. Not within. I'm not stepping into a new reality. I'm being stripped of my life and my feelings. Life has pulverised my memories and emotions and there's nothing left. I don't feel alive at all to be totally honest. I feel as though I'm changing into something that's so wrong

109

it can never be right. Like a robot. Do you understand?'

Petrov simply nodded.

'It makes sense. But only if you limit your contact with other people. Variety can break the scripted nature of things. What you are experiencing is part of the phenomenon I've been writing about, the speed and frequency of turmoil in modern life. People are experiencing profound shocks that leave them feeling that their lives might as well be a work of fiction. It's a kind of neurotic disorder. People used to be able to ignore these doubts as long as they felt their lives were moving in an upward direction; climbing the social ladder, owning property, having more choices and options. All that stuff. If I sacrifice my life my children will lead a better one. This doesn't happen so much these days. So what's the solution? People are coming to the conclusion that if you can't move up, move on. Move into another life. Upgrade to a newer version. The Internet has this immense transformative power. It provides access to self-knowledge like nothing else. As I said to you before it's about the speed, curiosity…and will.'

'Ok, so you think people like James get by, just by browsing the Internet by themselves?'

'Some do. Some don't. Or at least not without assistance. Allow me to show you. It might take years of remote monitoring to establish how the process of building up an individual's social identity is evolving. I am merely trying to establish cause and effects in a much more compressed timeframe. And this requires intervention of some kind by an artificially intelligent friend. I don't tell them what their choices are but the software programme, this one, Capucine, facilitates social situations and at varied rates of change for each person and advises them on common pitfalls, mistakes, how to take care of themselves.'

'By setting up situations?'

'More than that. By selecting and suggesting the right

emotional and social support mechanisms based on the individual's unique characteristics.'

Petrov prodded his tablet into life to bring up rows and columns of individual profile pictures on the big screen in front of us.

'Like these migrants to the UK or the student population of the university for example.'

He flicked between the two sets, swiping his screen one way and then the other, until he had picked out a face from the mosaic before us.

'You could choose any one of these individuals and without realising it they are all calibrating and re-calibrating themselves for something whether it's relationships, friendship, money and the rest. I am merely a single point in a larger network. I'm not the only one interested in this. Really, when I think about all the harm that your industry has done and is doing already.'

'What harm exactly?'

'You know. Harvesting data, infiltrating social networks, influencing decision making through the power of algorithms. It's been going on for years and in every election that comes round no-one seems to notice it. Our behaviour is already being influenced by data companies using AI to herd us into patterns of behaviour that they find useful. It's all behind the scenes. Your old business, advertising, have been doing the same thing for years. What we have so far failed to do is to make it something that people can use to serve their own lives. AI for the people by the people. The utopian vision of the digital world was one that empowered rather than enslaved…speaking of which….this is something I have been revisiting again. Here, you can have it. It's what this is all about.'

He handed me a book with the title *Walden Two* written in large letters on the cover. I tossed it between my hands like a hand grenade, wanting to throw it back at him.

'It isn't exactly my field anymore….I'm moving on from

all of that. I do recognize what you're saying but what exactly are you doing? Why don't you show me this Capucine? Who is she?' I said.

'The essence of what I have been doing for the last few years has been about the interaction between the individual and the world as mediated by an artificially intelligent third party. Call this third party the Internet, call it a form of super-consciousness, call it God if you want to. How would it be if this God knew your personality imprint and could present you with very specific information tailored to your individual tendencies and needs. It's still only the beginning. Imagine what it will be like in fifty years? The consciousness of being able to walk into a series of better versions of our lives will gain more momentum. Look at you for instance. Are you not a different man now to the one who nearly knocked me off the road? Eh?'

'It was you who nearly ran me into the motorway embankment, remember?'

'Was it? Maybe it was? Even so. It doesn't matter. What we are talking about is social and psychological pathways. A new kind of mirror.'

'Show me. Have you got Mark up on the screen there?'

Petrov swiped a few times to the right on his tablet and brought up Mark's picture. Then he tapped in a code and the TV screen on the wall filled with icons; personality, values, social-econ group, history. Petrov clicked into the history section and we were presented with a slowly evolving and changing series of words that he had typed into the search engine. Each presented itself on the screen as if it was a form of dialogue. Petrov noted something and looked further into the browsing history and search results.

'Look,' he said urging me to get closer to him, 'Capucine is listening and responding to his search behaviour. These results are not just tailored to him but are a reflection, like a mirror. Look, at his current behaviour. He's still evolving from using sex as a way to escape anxiety and loneliness.

112

This pathway is for someone who is unhappy with the quality of their relationships and wants to resolve their feelings about being lonely. It doesn't judge. But it does show you the negatives as well as the positives. It extracts the very best pre-selected pathways to help you to live well. Capucine holds a mirror up to the man. And unlike a real mirror, where we often change our facial expressions to suit what we want to see, she presents these men with how they actually are without judging them. I want to see if Mark can tap into a pathway and whether he will be more able to see the possibilities of the life beyond.'

This is about as much of the conversation as I can recollect, and I think it summarizes some of Petrov's views and his mission in life. I hope I've done some justice to it as he often talked at length about the subject. I have to confess that I felt troubled listening to him but would have been equally happy to have gone on late into the night, but I couldn't leave without giving him the photographs I'd taken of his research group. We hooked my camera into his screen and flicked through them one by one. He howled with excitement as we scrolled past one of James surrounded by his male counterparts and clapped with pleasure whenever we came across a relaxed and unbuttoned one of Mark or Steve, attempting to dance or throwing their heads back in laughter. Stella had done her job.

'Ha! Makes me feel slightly envious you know. I wish I had your skill with the camera. You're a natural director but I guess you must be tired. Don't let me keep you much longer.'

He reached into his jacket pocket for his wallet and counted out a slim volume of twenties.

'Two hundred for a job well done. Here.'

I took the money and folded it up in my back pocket.

'Well, I'll leave you to it then,' I said.

'I guess so,' he said and walked with me to the door, 'Thank you for your assistance. Let me know if you would like Capucine to help you.'

'I don't think so,' I said and turned to go.

'See you again Rich!'

And with that he closed the door and I felt bereft all of a sudden as if I had left behind a genial travelling companion at a station platform. I left wondering if we might be able to arrange to bump into one other further down the line.

12.

Internet Browsing History for 12th September

23.03 Snow Patrol – Chasing Cars - YouTube
23.13 Albert Camus on Suicide - Google Search
23.14 The Myth of Sisyphus - Wikipedia
23.16 Trip Advisor - WiKeeKee Reviews
23.22 Latest News, gossip and sport - Crunch News
23.23 Kate Winslett shows off her curves - Crunch News
23.26 E-Romantics - ElectrikTanya messaged you!

I planned to meet Matilda soon after my assignment with Petrov's men. Today was going to be the day. We'd arranged to meet at the *WiKeeKee* café on the beach. I got there early. As I waited I was served by a tall, blonde waitress with an Eastern European accent. She served me coffee and as she leaned over to serve me I caught a glimpse of her name tag which read 'Vivienne'. I thought back to when I last saw here at the airshow. I checked my phone for messages wondering all the while if I might come across her profile in Petrov's numerous followers. It didn't take long to find her and to get an idea of her age, (twenty-four), her relationship status (open), her university degree (biological sciences) and her interests (mountain biking, long distance cycling). Flowing from one photograph and one update to another helped pass the time and although I question myself now, I didn't question it at the time. Where does the addiction to this information come from? What use is it? Does our behaviour change when we have a window into someone's soul? I would never knowingly use any of it or admit to knowing it; until today. If anything it made me feel uneasy that it wasn't for the likes of me that she declares her love of mountains but companies like Wordfarm who will be using it to promote their clients' ranges of climbing boots or waterproof clothing. But it's remarkable that even a few basic details about her made me see her as more than another anonymous migrant and more respectful of her struggle to make her way in life.

And my struggle? Well, Anders has been stalling on my invitation to come down to the sea to visit me and I'm still waiting for news from the Real Image photo agency on some new work they'd initially sized up in Mumbai. Helen has not been in touch since our meeting in London and I wonder how things are working out with her new man. Of course, she's blocked me from her social networks and I have no way of following her, even from a distance. I had all but ignored the letter from her solicitor and just carried on with my life as before. I don't need any more flat pack furniture. Books? I'd taken the ones that meant something to me. Photographs? I stored them all digitally. I forget what other possessions I can lay claim to now. Power Tools? A Futon? Knowing Helen as I do I'm pretty sure that not all of them found their way to charity to await new owners. She has always been a collector.

As I scrolled through the messages on my phone I reopened one from *ElectrikTanya*. This girl, who had used a picture of a dog to advertise her personal brand, had got back to me yesterday from the dating site. Her message read:

Meunier? Is that really you? I thought you died in 1991? Get in touch.

I had fired back a reply with reference to Meunier's most infamous subject matter.

Oui ca va? You know zat I always prefer animal to human. Especially ze dog. Zey are so much more human that humans themselves.

No reply since yesterday and there was still no sign of

Matilda. I called her, but her mobile was switched off. I sent a message but nothing came back. After slurping at my cappuccino until there was no froth left I got up to pay the bill.

'I hope you don't mind me saying,' I began as Vivienne took my money.

'Yes?' she said.

'I used to go on assignment to Minsk occasionally. You're not Belorussian by any chance are you?'

'Yes! Amazing! Everyone assumes I am Polish but I'm not. How can you tell?'

'Intuition. A lucky guess.'

'Well, you have the luck that's for sure. And a nice smile.'

That's the first compliment I've received in a long, long time.

'Thank you.'

She smiled and shook her head in amazement as I left.

I left the *WiKeeKee* disappointed with Matilda's no-show. I'd been looking forward to speaking to her. I was ready to tell her all about Petrov and his outlandish theories. I wonder what she, a digital native, thinks of it all. I'd set up a couple of introductions to some of my professional friends in London. I'd have thought she'd have made an appearance even if it was only for that. I made my way back to the flat, back to the crumbling Victorian town-house by the sea with its endlessly repeating GIF of the tide going in and going out. I heard a ping from my phone. It was *ElectrikTanya*.

Are you a photographer monsieur?

All was silent on the landing outside the flat. I turned the key in the door whilst tapping a reply.

How did you guess? And you? Possibly a dog trainer or an artist?

Within seconds of getting into the flat I got another message.

Lol. Is it really so obvious?

The sound of the intercom broke the spell of what was

promising to be the start of a conversation. Someone was downstairs. I was slow to react. This wasn't the first time that the buzzer had been pressed by kids as they passed by. But then the buzzer sounded again. And again.

'Yes!' I said.

'Morning,' said a male voice.

'Yeah,' I replied.

'Delivery for flat next door. Let me in please.'

I was about to hit the key on the intercom when he interrupted.

'Let me in please.'

'Wait a second,' I said.

'What for? Just buzz me in. I will get a ticket.'

I opened the door of the flat and walked out into the hallway to my neighbour and knocked on the door.

I heard the sound of footsteps approaching and felt the sensation of being scrutinized through the fish-eye lens in the door. Seconds later I heard the turning of a key in the door. The fat-faced lady opened it, took a quick look at me and flung the door wide open, pulling me in. I wanted to tell her about the caller but she ushered me into the lounge and beckoned me to take a seat with an impressively wide smile.

'How can I help you my darling?' she began.

Her intercom began to buzz insistently. She ignored it and turned back to me.

'There's a guy trying to get into the building,' I said

'Oh God. Not again. Don't let him in,' she said and fumbled around for something in her cardigan, 'Excuse me while I take this call.'

She rushed out of the lounge into one of the bedrooms and closed the door behind her. The intercom continued to buzz. I walked over to it and was about to answer it when the young woman I'd encountered outside the flat the other day, the one who was shy and wouldn't entertain a coffee with me, emerged from the bathroom. Dressed in a white dressing gown she was combing her wet hair and without any sign of surprise she stopped and fixed her gaze on me carefully. When she heard the buzzer ring she just smiled and brought a finger to her lips.

'No answer,' she said.

The buzzer continued to sound.

'No answer,' she said.

He was starting to piss me off by now. Ill-tempered and foul mouthed I rushed back next door to fetch the Nikon then flung open one of the sash windows to get a good look at him. He was already looking upwards; a tall man, with arms that you could dent sheet metal with, a tattooed head and piercing eyes. I got some shots in quickly before he had time to react.

'Hey, who are you?'

'Why don't you do one before I call the police!' I said.

'Hey you. Give me pictures. Give me. I'll be back here. Don't think I'm walking away. I know your face and I know where you live. I'll be back for you and my girl.'

He crossed over to the other side of the street where I followed him with my lens. I could see him gesticulating and cursing to himself as he walked along the seafront. Like a comical super-villain he glanced back in my direction, stopped, wagged a finger at me and then resumed his walk as if being driven on by some demon. As I leaned back into the flat, I noticed a familiar car parked outside. It was Matilda. She was sitting at the wheel, looking down at her lap. Before I could wave to her she had started the engine and took off into the city. I checked my phone. She'd sent me a message.

'Hi, sorry I'm running late. Tied up with a client.'

And another

'Nearly finished. Will be with u soon.'

'Where are u?'

'Did you get my message?'

'I'll drive by your place to see if you're there.'

Perhaps due to some connectivity issues her text

119

messages had only just come through. That wasn't in the script. For the first time in a while I began to feel the pain of regret. I wasn't sure how to respond. I called her. Her phone was diverted to voicemail. I was frozen in time, not knowing what to say or how to say it with my heart flapping like a fish out of water. In any case I didn't have the luxury of being able to think for very long.

'Hello?' enquired a soft female voice from outside the flat, 'Hello?'

It was the fat lady next door. She had her fist raised as if she were about to knock but felt too afraid to. She smiled when I turned to face her.

'Hello, I'm sorry for all the trouble. May I come in?'

She pushed open the door and plodded into the studio.

'Yes,' I said, 'No need to apologise.'

'Oh but there is. I have no idea why that man keeps following us. This is the second flat we've moved to in the last few months and he keeps tracking us down. I am so sorry to have caused you so much trouble. I mean you're a nice man, trying to lead a peaceful life. You don't need people like me intruding and making it stressful for you. What can I do to make it up to you?'

'It's nothing. Really.'

'You're a gentleman. That's what Sabrina said about you.'

'Sabrina?'

'You met her once….outside on the stairs?'

'Ah yes,' I said.

'She's a lovely girl. She said you were very kind to her. She really liked you. Ahhh you have a studio. Are you an artist of some kind?'

'A photographer.'

'Perhaps I could give you some business my darling. Could I perhaps make you something to eat or drink? You look ever so famished and we're so grateful to you for getting rid of that awful man. Come on. Come next door.'

She was so kind and charming. She took my arm and led me back to her flat before I had time to react, but I had no intention of resisting her.

'My name is Rosetta darling. When you first came round I thought you were coming to introduce yourself to us? Would you like a bottle of wine for all your troubles? Please help yourself to something. We don't drink very much in this house. There's a bottle of champagne there if you'd like it. Help yourself to anything that takes your eye my love.'

I looked around her kitchen. It was smarter than mine and cleaner too. Rows of wine bottles had been stacked next to the fridge.

'No really that's OK,' I said.

'No, don't be shy,' she said reaching for a bottle of red and a white, 'Take these. Here, for you and perhaps you have a lady friend to share them with? No?'

She put them inside a plastic bag and handed it to me.

'Stay for a chat,' she said and squeezed my hand.

She made a coffee for everyone and we joined Sabrina in the lounge. Sabrina had dried her hair and had applied some make up. She smiled shyly and sipped her coffee as we sat down together to watch a news channel. Rosetta took the single armchair and encouraged me to sit next to Sabrina on the sofa.

'Sabrina always insists on catching up with this silly news, CNN, Al-Jazeera and that kind of thing. Don't you Sabrina? I'm not all that interested. I prefer a good drama instead of all these numbers. I mean what do they all mean?'

I looked at Sabrina.

'I prefer business. And money. And it helps me to improve my English,' she said.

'I notice you've improved a lot since we last met,' I replied.

'I study at the university.'

Rosetta began chuckling to herself, 'She never speaks English if she doesn't want to chat. Isn't that so darling?'

'Sometimes is better if you don't talk to strangers,' said Sabrina.

'But he's not a stranger to us. He's a friend,' said Rosetta.

'What are you studying?' I asked.

'Business and journalism. At the university here. I want to get a good English degree and work in City of London. For Bloomberg or financial news company.'

'That's good. Where are you from?'

'Slovenia,' she said.

'There's a lecturer at the university I know. I think he's from your part of the world. Nikola Petrov? Do you know him?'

'Yes. He's is doing some work for me.'

'For you?'

'Yes. Let me show you.'

Sabrina turned on the interface on her wrist watch. A friendly face appeared on the display. 'Hello Sabrina,' it said.

'This is Cassian. He is an angel. Protecting woman against abuses. The professor is trialling it with me and some of the other girls in the university.'

'What does he do?'

'He blocks out abusive messages, texts, social media. He's a bot. He can also delete harmful contents about me online. I never get any abuses online. No threats. No violence. He can also notify me if someone is following me.'

'How? Do you mean stalking?'

'Yes. Stalking. That's exactly what I mean. This guy. The one you saw outside has been stalking me since I left home. He follows me but with Cassian I can see where he is. How close. How far away.'

She brought the device closer to my face so that I could see. She swiped a couple of screens and moved to a Sat Nav displaying the city map with a moving red dot.

'There. That's him. Moving away.'

'But never far enough I imagine. He'll be back.'

Sabrina shrugged her shoulders and began combing her

hair.

'If I say a code word Cassian immediately begins dialling the police and speaks to them on my behalf, forwarding my exact location to their computers.'

'That should be on the market. I'd happily go back into advertising for something like that.'

'Well, I think that's the idea,' she shrugged.

We watched the news channel for half an hour where they were chatting about the generally parlous condition of the Asian markets before finishing our coffee. I left them in peace to get on with things and by the time I'd got back to my flat and put away the bottles of wine I remembered Matilda.

I called her but there was no answer. I sent her a text:

Sorry I missed you earlier. Got tied up with helping a neighbour with a nuisance caller. All a bit strange. Talk to you later.

I went back to my work editing the photos from a shoot near Manchester for a yoghurt maker; all hills, fields, cows and sexy young farmers but I could feel the pull of the Internet as I worked, tempting me with its possibilities; the golden promise of its never ending discourse. I looked for *ElectrikTanya* once again. She'd sent me a new message:

Do you want to come to the Lucien Freud exposition this weekend? You can meet some of my friends. Would be G8 to meet you. Tanya. x

I didn't know what to do. If I replied to Tanya it had to be in the affirmative. To do otherwise would probably mean I'd never hear from her again. This was a new script inviting me to play my part. Petrov's lecture to me on the natural causes of man's social isolation came to mind. I wanted to escape my cold, robotic isolation and this invitation opened up the possibility of deviating from this path. Petrov had said that stepping into a parallel life wasn't easy. There was Matilda of course but I felt that something had already passed me by in my relationship with her. I returned to my computer screen and typed a response:

123

I'd love to come along. How will I recognize you?

Later that night, much later, after I had been browsing the Internet for hours following the career of one narcissistic soul after another, I received another message. It was Matilda.

Can't wait to hear about it... Lol. Can't meet tonight but see you next week?

I put the phone to one side and continued browsing. Just as I was about to turn off the laptop I checked the dating site for new messages. ElectrikTanya had buzzed me again.

Simple. I am the curator. I will meet you at the entrance. If you send me your real name I will recognize you when you sign in.

It didn't sound like a date.

13.

Internet Browsing History 17th September

08.07 Lucien Freud - Waldegrave Museum - Google Search
08.08 Waldegrave Museum - About Us
08.12 Waldegrave Museum - Meet the Curators - Tanya Lopez
08.16 Tanya Lopez - Linkedin -Google Search
08.17 Tanya Lopez - Denver Journal of Orthodontists
08.18 nikpetrov2000 - Twitter
08.25 TED Talks - Strategies for Better Conversations

I arrived at the Waldegrave Museum early. I'd put on my dirty white pumps and crumpled pin-striped suit and had taken Petrov's advice on abstinence to heart, resisting the urge to down a few glasses of the old Pisco before heading out. I was a bag of nerves. I must have walked the streets around the gallery a dozen times, stopping to look in at the windows of women's fashion boutiques and jewellers, staring at the prices of heirlooms long passed on from their first or even second owners. The one emotion that I could have wished my cybernetic self to have extinguished was fear. This insidious and underhand emotion has never taken leave of me when all other tender emotions have. I very nearly sent a message to Tanya to propose another date so that I wouldn't have to meet other people. Going home to work on my collection of photographs seemed pleasantly alluring. I thought about giving it another half an hour to ensure that the venue would already be filled with people. The idea of simply walking into the gallery seemed impossible. As I turned around to make another circuit I froze again in front of another shop window.

I looked at myself in the glass. I still thought of myself as a machine; a processor of life's experiences; a data-mining ant in a hive of information. If that were true, I thought, it follows that I must be able to use data to re-programme myself. If I was going through the motions, reading from a script, then might I not be able to change the script or at least rewrite it until it could have an alternative influence on my life. I tried. Surely meeting a woman in an art gallery and failing to connect with her was foreseeable and therefore predictable. If it was a predictable outcome based on my age and recent relationship breakup then it was more than likely to be meaningless. Yes, I argued back, but the desire to connect with people needn't be meaningful. What meaning do our relationships have apart from accidental ones? Let this be an accident. If I didn't like her and she didn't like me, so what? My insides still felt as still and about as stable as a crisp packet billowing on the wind. As I looked into the shop window, I noticed a dark-haired mannequin with brown staring eyes, dressed from top to toe in a long black evening gown. It was Petrov's mannequin, the model for Capucine, now working as a model in a charity shop. I could have sworn it was her.

I forced myself back around the block until I was outside the entrance to the Waldegrave. Inside I was greeted by a giant stiff-necked lady with long, grey hair stretching down to the small of her back. She leaned towards me like a giraffe leaning towards a branch.

'Good evening, do you have your invitation please?'

I showed her the ticket that Tanya had emailed.

'Lovely. Could you also give me your name please?'

I gave it. She pored over a clipboard with a broken pen until she found it.

'Mr. Kidd. If you'd like a glass of wine please help yourself from the table over there. I hope you enjoy the exhibition.'

My attention wasn't fully on the grey lady. I stared over

her shoulder looking for Tanya. The place was rammed with quaffing socialites and other pretenders to high culture.

'Is there anything else I can help you with?' said the grey lady.

'No, no, that's fine. Just wondering where to start.'

'Take your pick but if I were you I'd start with the dogs over there.'

I picked up a glass of red before turning around to face the paintings. Most people had congregated around the middle of the room where they could avoid the art altogether. It was as scripted as any of the opening nights I'd ever been to. I turned my back on the sweating mass of people to take it all in. It was a large space with high ceilings and wooden floors in the shape of a large rectangle. I looked at my phone to find Tanya. She'd checked in alright but all I knew was that she was somewhere in the room. I spotted a woman wearing a white name tag who was busy in conversation with a group near me. I couldn't read the name tag from where I was standing but her trout pout and orange skin made me dread finding out. It was then that I noticed a bald head and dark glasses bobbing away in another corner of the room. Unmistakably it was Petrov. He was with a coterie of grey hairs, academics like himself presumably, gesticulating and explaining some sociological point about Freud's portrayal of the ball sack no doubt. I was tempted to go over and say hello but I knew that I'd never get away. There seemed nothing for it but to hang around and look at the paintings. I turned back to face the wall and stare at the first set of naked portraits. Then, I noticed a new entrant to the room; a dark haired woman wearing a grey Trilby and a bright red flower in the lapels of her jacket. She spoke to the grey lady, who checked her clipboard and pointed in my direction. Pretending not to notice I waited until she got close enough to tap me on the shoulder.

'Hello, Richard?' she said with a bright smile.

'Tanya?'

'Glad you could make it. I was worried you weren't going to show up.'

Her voice had a distinct Latin swing.

'Well. I had some work to do at the studio. You know how things are with clients. Deadlines, deadlines,' I said.

'Tell me about it. I get these calls from high society women who want a piece of art for the entrance to the house. They ask me for advice. What do they want me to tell them? How to use their own eyes? It's impossible.'

'They're more concerned about their own image than what's in front of them.'

'Exactly. You like?' she said.

'Yes, I do. Did you organize this?'

'With a little help from my friends. You know this has been a fantastic project. I always love British art and to get so close to the paintings, how they were created, how long the sitters had to wait for a finished piece was amazing. And I got to meet the artist which was wonderful. Such an interesting man.'

I liked Tanya from the beginning. She had a pretty smile, eyes that seemed inviting and a pointed, dimpled chin. She was quite short, and I imagined she was quite slender judging by the way her trouser suit seemed to cloak her body.

'Look, behind you Richard,' she went on, 'Do you see the girl reclining on the chair. She has very wide hips but a small face. Angry and full of angles. She was only twenty-three or twenty-four when this was painted. Now look at the photograph of her below. She was a very beautiful girl no?'

I looked at the photograph and then the painting and back again at the photo, but I wasn't really concentrating.

'He transformed her into something else,' I said.

'Exactly. You see the resemblance but at the same time he has taken an especial mood or character of the girl and

128

brought it out to the front.'

'Something of a soul sifter,' I said but I don't think she got it. Something was lost in translation and she looked confused.

'Do you have a favourite British artist Richard?'

'Well, to be honest with you I find British art a bit too brutal….you know….too harsh. I prefer photography. There's more elegance to it.'

She laughed at me.

'What? What's funny'

'You never like your own art. It's so funny but you always prefer something else. I suppose you like Cartier-Bresson?'

'And Annie Leibovitz.'

Tanya smiled and looked around the room.

'Shall we meet my friends?' she asked but without waiting for a reply, 'Come. Come with me. They are really nice.'

I followed her as she danced around the shifting crowd, past Petrov and his chums, to the other side of the gallery. She turned around to assure herself that I was still following. I looked up to see a large art instillation, a spider made of car tyres, suspended directly above me. A vision of cables snapping and the ceiling giving way came into my head and the spider mercifully landing on me, crushing me to death.

'Richard, this way,' said Tanya, beckoning me to come on like a child leading a friend to the bottom of the garden.

I poked my head around the last group of gallery vultures before seeing a trio of scruffy men chatting beneath a picture of a man asleep with his dog. They failed to take any notice until Tanya poked her head into the middle of the discussion and pulled me into the circle.

'Okay, let me introduce you to everybody. First, this is Pablo. He's an artist as well and Colombian. Then there's Romain, he's a student from France and Pavel who's from

Poland, is working to becoming an architect. And guys this is Richard, who's a photographer and you are English no?' she said, touching each man in turn as she introduced them.

'Hello Richard, how do you like the exhibition?' asked Pablo, a giant moon-faced man with thick strands of hair parted down the middle and a beard trimmed to a point. Everyone else nodded and looked in my direction.

'I'd be feeling a bit more comfortable if I didn't have to stare at a pair of balls or arseholes everywhere I look,' I said.

It raised a laugh.

'Richard, you will need to cover Tanya's ears because this not my idea of beauty. Not this. The women of this country have such a big ass.'

'You haven't been to Colombia,' said Pablo.

'Well look at this one, he's pulling his legs so far apart you could fit a train up there,' said Romain.

'Or he's waiting to have a colonoscopy,' I said.

'No,' said Pablo, 'This one has already had the colonoscopy.'

'Oh, you are so horrible,' said Tanya, 'You said you liked it.'

'We do, we do,' added Pablo.

'Yes, you did very well,' said Pavel, 'I never knew much about this artist before.'

Tanya turned to me and smiled, 'They think they can fool me, but they are just pretending to dislike it.'

'The Pirelli spider up there,' I said, 'who did that?'

'That one. That's an installation by a local artist. Her name is Lisa Allbeury. She's very good. I think you'd like her. She also did something with a mannequin made out of circuit boards. Quite a frightening piece. You should come further down the gallery to see it.'

'I don't like this spider much,' said Pablo, 'but I like her dolls.'

'Tanya,' said Pavel, 'I wish I knew more about art. Can you teach me?'

'I would love to teach you Pavel, but you don't need a teacher. You just need to spend enough time around art to appreciate it,' said Tanya.

Pablo was scratching his beard and interrupted before Pavel could speak.

'What you need to know is...that you don't really need to know anything about the technicalities of the painting.'

'But I find it interesting,' insisted Pavel.

'Interesting,' Pablo went on, 'But irrelevant. You don't need to know anything about it unless you're a freak like Tanya who loves this kind of thing.'

'No, no, no, I disagree' said Pavel, 'Some of these pieces of art don't make any sense.'

'With photography it's clearer,' I said, 'especially if you're dealing with people. Whenever I've worked with photographers I find that you tend to get a lot of very different reactions from a person during a photoshoot. Most of them are unusable so you attempt to....play a game with your audience by only choosing those images that hit the mark. In advertising you can channel those reactions until you're confident you have the reaction you want. Art's more opaque. More interesting to interpret.'

'You work in advertising?' said Pablo.

'Used to. I was one of the lucky ones who escaped.'

'No? There is no escape my friend.' said Romain.

'I gave it up to move here.'

'You gave up a job in advertising in London?' said Pablo, 'Are you crazy?'

'Pablo, can't you see,' said Romain, 'He is breathing the pure air now, escaping from the capitalist monster, starting a new life. No, sorry but please continue with your escape attempt. Don't mind my friend. He can be very direct. What adverts did you create?'

'Atlantis, Fidel, Pisco Sour' I said

'You did those?' asked Pablo in amazement.

'Yes,' I said.

'Sorry but they were good,' said Pablo.

'Yes, well selling stuff isn't everything. The industry is changing now. It's all about the data. Big data. Small data. Your data,' I said turning to face Tanya, but she had already moved on to another group and was being introduced to a well-to-do ensemble made up of boutique dresses and silk ties.

'Tuh!' said Romain, 'Mannequins!'

'Patrons of the arts,' Pablo commented.

Romain chuckled to himself and drew us onto the subject of Hugo Chavez. 'Do you think he spent any of that oil money on art?'

Pablo bristled.

I felt a tap on my shoulder. It was Tanya.

'Would you like me to show you around?' she said.

I followed Tanya through the crowd until we reached the far corner of the gallery. It wasn't what I was expecting; Lisa Allbeury's mannequin. It was a female, with the weight of its body leaning slightly on one leg with the other pointing forward. She had a hand nestled on one of her hips and was naked from head to foot. Her skin was only partially exposed though as much of the surface of her body was covered in visual images and what can only be described as chips and circuits from computers or phones. The mannequin was bald and for good reason, allowing us to see a section of her head which had been cut away to reveal a set of circuit boards instead of a brain surmounted with a tiny device. A bomb? The so-called biological clock? Her cheek was covered in advertisements for skincare and anti-ageing products, the right side of the brain with foreign language newspapers and political comment. Across her chest she bore personal health information about her body mass index and diet. In her armpits dangled the telephone numbers of various men. Her stomach was covered in dietary advice and the names of various restaurants and cook books. Her ribs were glued with deadlines for yoga and cycling classes and the other side of her rib cage with images of faces and words written on social networking sites. The space between her legs was covered with a giant fig leaf shape cut from a magazine article on *20 Ways to Enjoy Better Sex*. Glancing down at her legs revealed that she wore a pair of glittering red shoes just like Dorothy in the Wizard of Oz. There was also a child reaching up to the hand that was hanging by her side. This child was some Renaissance cherub cut from a classical work of art and gazing up at the hand with unswerving devotion. The hand, always within reach, was decorated with feathers which drew my attention to the other hand again. I glanced across to discover that the hand on the mannequin's hip had hooked claws for finger nails.

It was an effort just examining the work.

'You get tired from looking at it? Imagine what it's like being a woman,' said Tanya.

'Or any human being in the modern world,' I said.

Tanya clapped her hands together excitedly, 'I knew you would like it. Pablo thinks he understands it, but he just doesn't get it. He thinks it's about women repressing their sexual desires. That's not what Lisa is saying at all.'

'How about you?' I said, 'Do you have anything on display here?'

'No, not here but in my studio and also back in Spain. I want to try to get something exhibited here. I paint in a very simple way. People, always two people at a time because I like to bring together how they are with each other. It's very difficult to explain to you. And you?'

'Crowds and their emotions. I try to go to places where there are lots of people; events, concerts, sports. Crowds are going to be the new wave.'

'Are you exhibiting?'

'No, I need to find a gallery too.'

Tanya touched me on the forearm for a brief moment and laughed.

133

'You know, we could work together to find one. You have similar problems to me I think.'

I smiled and felt the urge to reach out and touch her. Instead I looked into her eyes to find them inspecting me curiously.

'Shall we get back to your friends?'

'Yes, of course,' she said, 'We mustn't neglect them. They will be missing us.'

They were happy to see us; Pablo put his arm around Tanya and gave her a big hug.

'What are we going to do without you?' he said.

'Yes, when are you going back to Spain?' asked Pavel.

'I am going back in a couple of weeks. It will be sad to leave you guys, but I haven't made up my mind about coming back just yet.'

'The situation is bad everywhere,' said Romain, 'Stay with us.'

'You could always stay to put on an exhibition of your own work or we could work together,' I said. I forgot about the script. Or was that what the script wanted me to say?

'Yes!' said Pablo patting me on the shoulder. 'Now we are talking. He can persuade people to like your stuff. He can get people to buy anything. Ha Ha.'

I stayed for another hour. Tanya began to tell me about herself. She told me she was from Madrid. Her mother was a Tunisian immigrant and her Spanish father ran a business in the city. She studied in Madrid, worked as a tourist guide, lived with her brother Antonio in an apartment in the city and painted in her spare time. She moved to England following the financial crisis to get work. Slowly, I began to sense that the evening was beginning to peter out. The crowds had shrunk, and the paintings now loomed ever larger in the increasingly empty vault of the gallery. I took it as a sign that I should go too. As I said goodbye she insisted on kissing me on both cheeks. I inhaled her perfume and as I write this I can still catch the scent of her.

'Call me ok?' she whispered. Her friends shook my hand and wished me luck.

Outside the gallery I realised just how close I had come to being in jeopardy, a feeling that this might have gone badly wrong and one of surprise at myself that I had somehow managed to navigate my way through it. I was giddy with adrenalin and wine and I tottered off to find my way back to the flat shambling down the wrong street. I looked in at the shops, looked in at the people enjoying themselves in bars and then walked back down the seafront to kick my way along the beach and look out to sea. My head was full of chaotic impressions from the evening. I checked the phone in my jacket pocket. It was Matilda.

Hi, are u around tomorrow eve for drinks?

It feels entirely farcical that I might now have to face the dilemma of letting someone down. When I finally reached the homestead and closed the door of the flat behind me, I poured myself a glass of the old Pisco Sour and wrote Matilda a reply.

Good thx. U? how about 8 at the PumpRms?

Did I do well?

14.

Internet Browsing History 18th September

11.59 Lavapies - Google Search
00.01 Google Image Results -Un barrio catizo/ lavapies/ Tursimo
00.02 Google Image Results - www.rentalapartlavapies/ street.jpg
00.03 Lavapies - Wikipedia
00.06 Google Maps - Street View - Calle de Valencia
00.08 Search - Lisa Allbeury's Woman
00.10 Evening Standard - Why Allbeury's Woman is
00.21 Account Sign-in - Cyberneticgreeneyes - Message Box
00.28 How to let someone down gently - Real School of Life

After the previous fiasco I made a few somewhat lazy online enquiries to my old professional network. I pinged a few messages recommending Matilda to a diverse range of people from former contacts at the Wittchety Grub to anyone who I thought might owe me a favour. I'd forgotten about many of these people, lying dormant in my online network like a family tree that you roll up and forget about until you come across it by chance in a drawer or in a box in the attic. Some wrote back with messages of false hope; 'I'd love to help but we're full at the moment. I'll keep her details on file.' Bastards all. It was all strangely moving. I hadn't expected to feel so disappointed and angry on Matilda's behalf. Undeterred I phoned up the one grand dame of advertising recruitment that I knew might help. The problem was that she could be a bitch. I called her after eleven when I knew she'd have downed enough coffee to take a bath in.

'Oh Richard. So lovely to hear from you. What are you

doing with yourself these days? Still having a sabbatical?'

'Yes, still working on stuff. I've got projects coming out of my ears,' I said.

'Oh, I know. You creative minds can't help yourselves. Have you been in touch with anyone at Wordfarm recently?'

'You know. I've been so busy lately that I haven't been in touch.'

'Well it's all going tits up. The end of year results came out last week and they were pretty grim. My phone hasn't stopped ringing. They either want to jump ship or have already been told they're up for the chop. They'll be laying off staff all over the place. I've been bombarded but there's just not much out there. So heartbreaking. You got out at the right time Rich.'

'Have you heard anything about my old crew?'

'I haven't heard from them. Tom would have been in touch if they were threatened. He keeps asking me to find you some work. Are you sure I can't help you?'

'Yes, you might be able to. Did you get my email about Matilda?'

'Oh yes. Lovely name. Lovely picture. I do like one of those old-fashioned names. I'm not sure I've got much for her. No experience.'

'She's very bright. What about social media? She'd be amazing at that. She practically runs the social media wing of the property firm she's at. That's how I got my place down here.'

'It's very competitive. So many graduates go for these things. But as it's you I'll put her to the front of the queue my lovely.'

'Thank you! Let me know if you need me for anything.'

'Can't you set up your own firm Rich and start hiring people!'

I arrived late for the Pump Rooms. It made no difference. She arrived half an hour late anyway. By then I'd already drained my cappuccino cup right down to the bottom and had buried myself in the book review section on my tablet.

Petrov. N. The Human Crash of 2050

'Sorry!' she said, 'I got caught up with another last minute booking and then I had to go all the way back across town to get changed. Mum had some problems with her car and she dragged me into helping her. Did you get my message?'

She was cold. Her hands and nose were red, and she sniffed as she pulled off her coat and set her bag down on the table.

'No. I mean I don't think so. I can check, just a minute,' I said closing down the websites on my tablet.

'No, it's OK. I'm just wanted to say I'm reeeeeeelly sorry! I couldn't get out of it. Mum's such a nightmare when she gets herself into a state. Can I get you a drink of anything?'

'No, let me,' I said.

'Don't be silly. I got a message from a very nice lady in London. She's got me an interview next week. It's the least I can do.'

'Ok. A tea would be nice.'

Beaming with pleasure she clip-clopped her way to the baristas to order our drinks. She practically dwarfed everyone in the queue even in her flat shoes. I remembered how attractive she is when she's in a retro mood. Gone was the 1950's California girl of yesterday. In came the 1940's munitions girl. She was wearing a tightly wound headscarf around her hair and a pale denim blue shirt. Bright red lipstick and mascara brought it all together. If I hadn't known better I'd have thought she was auditioning for a role. There was definitely something of the performer in her.

'Do you take sugar?' she asked.

I shook my head.

'Right,' she said and got back to the waitress.

She looked and sounded every inch a girl-woman as she asked for gluten free cakes as if she were shopping for an allergic son or daughter. When she returned to our table, she snapped her handbag open and began to rummage around for something.

'So, tell me. How are you?' I said.

'Really happy about the news. Thank you. Sorry about last time. I really thought you might be angry with me because you didn't return my calls. When I drove over to your flat it all looked a bit scary and surreal. Who was that guy?'

'Him? Oh. A nasty piece of work. He's stalking the girl in the flat next door. He tried to force his way in. He hadn't bargained on me having a camera to film his outburst.'

'That's very gallant of you. Do you know this girl?' she asked.

'Only to say hello to.'

'Is she young? Pretty?' said Matilda, widening her eyes at me.

'Well, yes. All of those things. Why are you looking at me like that?'

'Nothing,' said Matilda, 'I just wondered if you'd even noticed her. She's bound to be interested in you now that you've saved her. Didn't she invite you over?'

'Well, yes. She did. But nothing happened,' I added.

'I wouldn't have judged you if it had,' laughed Matilda.

The waitress came over to set down two pots of tea, a brownie and two sets of tea cups and saucers.

'Thank you so much for helping me,' said Matilda, 'I know it's only an interview, but I can't tell you how excited I am by this. It's right up my street.'

'Honestly, I didn't really do anything. It was you.'

'Well,' she said, 'I don't mind admitting that I don't feel all that secure. I'm scared about the future.'

'Sometimes I feel just like that. Something inside me is

139

saying 'don't do it!' I can't explain it better than that.'

'It's like everything is acting upon everything else. Like you coming down here to search for a flat. And now we're here. Shall we go to see a film tonight? There's a new Spanish one at the Arts Centre. According to my phone it starts in about an hour.'

'Why not? I love reading subtitles.'

Matilda wagged her finger at me.

We finished off in the café and walked towards the Arts Centre. We linked arms on the way. I insisted on buying the tickets. We had only just made it and as the lights dimmed we shuffled along in the dark to find our seats. Both of us are very tall and so we were very cramped in our seats with our thighs and knees pressed against each other. The film got underway and we were introduced to the main character. He was a slick Parisian of sorts, a financier for a major international bank who had the gift of being able to play his hand with an artfulness that bordered on manipulation. The rest of his life was a mess as he bumbled around with professional women setting up dates which never seemed to go anywhere. Bored he drifts off into the murky world of late-night jazz bars and strip clubs. There he meets a man who offers to find him a woman. The man is a Russian gangster who has confused our hero with a pimp. The real pimp, we learn, has already been assassinated on his way to the meeting. Our hero's dilemma is whether or not to continue with the pretence of negotiation as the Russian begins to try to force a deal for a woman he wants to get rid of. He goes ahead with it as it piques his professional pride and buys the woman almost as a private joke. But this isn't a joke. The seriousness of the situation dawns on him once he is taken to see the girl and he begins a deadly game with the Russians to hold on to his life and free the woman from her bondage. The woman is driven to our hero's apartment which is assumed to be his safe house for trafficked women. Once he has the girl in his possession he explains the situation to her and they begin a deadly game of pretence.

I could see; even in the dim light that Matilda was gripped. The plot was a little bizarre for my tastes but the impending threat of violence and promise of romance kept me hooked. Buyer and slave hatch a brilliant plan together to negotiate their way out by secretly filming the Russian gangsters and a prominent French politician in compromising situations. And so, the two characters end up extorting enough money to cancel the debt and make an escape to the border where at a station they go their separate ways across the Alps to new lives.

As the credits punched the screen like an immigration officer punching a passport I looked over at Matilda. She wrinkled her nose and wiped her eyes.

'Were you crying?'

'A bit,' she said.

'I don't know why it got to me so much. I'm not the type of person to cry at films. I was hoping the two characters might have got together at the end.'

'It would have been more romantic but not very realistic.'

'That's my kind of romantic.'

'Well, the film leaves it open to interpretation. Perhaps they'll become friends on Facebook and hook up later.'

Matilda laughed. 'Is that the ending you would prefer?'

'Well sometimes the friendships you have with people are better than a full relationship. Fewer disappointments.'

The crowd began shuffling out of their seats and out through the exits. As we got out into the fresh air it was dark and a cold wind was blowing in off the sea. We drifted away from the Arts Centre and down the steps of the City Hall.

'Well, what now?' asked Matilda.

'I don't know about you but I'm totally exhausted,' I said, 'I think I'm going to hit the sack.'

'Will you be OK getting home?'

'Yeah, don't worry. I can look after myself. I'll send you a text when I get in. Well, good night then,' I said and leaned in to give her a hug and to kiss her on both cheeks.

'It was nice evening,' she went on, 'Now don't go all silent on me. There's always Facebook. And let me know when you get your exhibition up and running because I want to be there.'

So, that's how it went. I wandered the long and winding lanes all the way back to the flat, drank a couple of shots of the old Pisco and flicked between the titillating lifestyle programmes scheduled in for people who can't or won't sleep. Something about *The World's Heaviest Man* stopped me from hopping to the next channel. Perhaps it was his bright, smiling Mexican face. This man, for whom the term morbidly obese was less than a description more a definition of the term, should never had made his mother cry like this and was surprisingly chirpy. He was also getting married for a second time. *'I am proof you can find love in any circumstances,'* he said as he was carted to the wedding ceremony on a truck. As the credits rolled I found it difficult to control myself. I could scarcely believe that what I was seeing was true and yet I have to confess I shed a few tears and cried like I hadn't cried for a long time.

15.

It's happened. I've made the transition to what I feared I might become when the old life was jettisoned. Now I see the new one starting to take shape. The cybernetic man is no longer a dream. He's a reality. I am now, more than ever plugged into the machine. My daily routines of emailing and browsing for work in my small studio are mere functional duties. The vast undiscovered country of the Internet sits on the very fringes and borders of my waking mind and is at all times beckoning me to step forward. Every moment in front of a keyboard carries with it a certain submission to its elevated ideals that any number of my needs might be satisfied within its borders. I am learning and faltering at the same time. It's an effort. Constantly linking with others, connecting, interacting with them and taking the time to check and re-check their responses. It's surprising that I get any work done. For all the work it involves this online slavery is helping me to get a few photography gigs. But every so often those pauses and silences in front of the keyboard begin to seem longer and heavier. And in those moments of silence I hear the Siren call of another world, beckoning me down another passageway or through another field, round another door and through another window. 'Do you want me?' it breathes lustily in my ear. Putting the earphones in is no defence. No matter how much of my time is taken from me I can't resist. And when I am 'liked', when I am 'shared' with the group I feel something cool and replenishing lubricating the pathways and tubes that run to my little heart. I am supposedly connected and yet, at the same time I don't feel part of things. Plugged in seems a far better description. The problem with the analogy is that it naturally leads me to consider what happens when I'm unplugged; will I cease to function? Do I dare let go?

I hadn't expected the tears. It wasn't just the fat Mexican's plight that got me, but he acted as a gateway to something else. The memories flooded back of Helen; Helen laughing, Helen cycling through countryside, Helen cooking, Helen pulling funny faces at me as her train set off for home and I waited on the platform. They were all still there, as vibrant and as colourful as they'd always been and hadn't been completely erased. It took me by surprise and I cried for them, the first time that I've shed any tears in some time. I can see that something needs to change but I feel stranded. I needed to see Petrov. I'd finally got that article published about him in a creative mag.

I caught up with him at the college. I sent him a message and he replied swiftly with a straightforward instruction, 'Meet me outside the Isaiah Berlin Lecture Hall. I finish at 2.30.' I'd never seen him in his arena of expertise before and looked up the building's location on my phone. I arrived perhaps fifteen minutes early, parking up by a collection of nineties college buildings built in a semi-circular arc of brick and glass. I walked across a well-tended lawn and followed a line of young saplings, all arranged in parallel lines, towards the main entrance. Inside the block I searched for a reception desk but there were only crowds of students flowing through the corridors. I wondered if I might catch a glimpse of Sabrina. I haven't seen her around the flat recently. I followed the signs to the Isaiah Berlin and saw from a red light outside the door that Petrov's lecture was still in progress. No surprise that it was over-running. Bloody Petrov. He took ages. When the doors finally swung open a troop of student bodies flowed out into the corridor. At one point I thought I noticed Sabrina's blonde ponytail swaying behind her. She didn't turn around so I couldn't say for sure that it was her. Finally, Petrov emerged looking relaxed, sporting a new earring and a new pair of yellow-tinted specs.

'Richard,' he growled, 'So glad to see you. You haven't been in touch for a long time. Everything going well? How's the photography? Come on. Let's catch up. We can't stand around in the corridor like this. Why don't we go up to my room and I can drop this off? It's just up these stairs. Tell, me how is everything going? Any news?'

'I'm earning a living. What more is there to say? Some friends are helping me out with work here and there.'

'Funny you should mention that. Networks. That's just what I've been lecturing about. The rise and fall of networks. Sometimes you're in. Sometimes you're out. The range and scope are incredible and it's increasing exponentially. Without networks you are almost like a Robinson Crusoe figure trying to survive on an island.'

'If only Crusoe had wi-fi,' I said.

'Exactly!' replied Petrov, 'If Crusoe had wi-fi he could've issued his cry for help on social media. Not that anyone would have done anything apart from re-post his message. You need to go beyond that. But networks have their place if you can tap into their customs and hierarchies. But outsiders beware. This is a club.'

'True. I'm only getting the work because of who I know. The strange thing is that ever since I dropped out so many of the people I knew have disappeared as if they've been wiped off the face of the planet.'

'That's very typical. There's an inherent series of biases in the network system towards power and interest,' Petrov went on, puffing slightly as we reached the top of the stairs and turning a corner towards a row of office doors, 'Once you understand them you can work to overcome some of them. And I have to emphasise the point - some of them, some of the time. The advantage of the digital world is that you have access to a plurality of networks that is much wider both geographically and socially than the real world. New networks are being baptised at a faster rate than

Catholics. You can always create one that's more to your liking, but I expect you didn't come to hear a summary of my lecture.'

'No,' I said.

'Well, here we are.'

We arrived outside his office, fronted by a plain white door with a plaque bearing his name. He pulled a set of keys out of his pocket and fiddled with the lock, opening the door on a small but perfectly proportioned square room lined with bookcases.

'Come in, make yourself comfortable. Would you like a glass of something?'

'No thanks,' I said and took a seat in one of two egg shaped chairs that I supposed served as perches for his students.

Petrov placed his laptop down on top of his desk and rather than sit behind it he opened the venetian blinds to let some more light into the room before shifting his posterior to the desk itself, leaning against it and waiting silently for me to return to the thread of our conversation.

'How are your students doing?' I said.

'The students are the incubators of all the new theories and practices of digital sociology. They are living and breathing it. They were born into what people like you and me still regard as a dual world. To, them there is no such thing as analogue and digital. It's all one.'

'Sorry, I meant your other students. Mark, James. How are they?'

Petrov smiled. 'Why don't you come along and find out? They'd like to see you again.'

'Likewise. I haven't really heard much from them since I sent their photos.'

'You mean you haven't connected with them yet?'

I didn't know what to say

'Well, it doesn't matter. We're very nearly at the end of this particular cycle of research now. The men are getting ready to move on. The parallel versions of their lives are beginning to open up. Come along. How's the rest of your life going?'

'Well I've met someone I like. I really need to try to meet her again before she goes back to Spain.'

'A girl? Excellent,' said Petrov, 'If you don't mind me asking why is she going back to Spain and why aren't you going with her?'

'That's the problem. I'm late. Too late. I met her when she'd already booked her flights. She's finished her time at the museum here and she's off home.'

Petrov nodded.

'Then make her want to stay. The past has all but gone but what's to replace it?' he said tapping his head, 'Think of what's next. Once you start living in the future you'll find that all your old emotions return. Like new. So, keep asking yourself, 'What do I want? What am I doing?' Look, you're very welcome to come to my next session with the guys. It's tonight. Why don't you come along? I'd be interested to know what you think.'

I wasn't sure. I didn't really want to discover that James, computer literate but illiterate in so many of life's other arts and sciences, had become an amusing pastiche of the man he might prefer to be. Could the Internet, acting as demi-god to its citizens, be trusted to educate? Petrov seemed to sense that something was up.

'Is that the magazine article?' he said.

I showed it to him.

'Good, very good,' he said, 'They've not bastardised my words too much. The essence is there, and you've made me look far cooler than I am. I owe you a favour. Let me buy you a drink.'

I caved in. All that Petrov would tell me was that we'd be doing some late-night shopping and asked me to meet him at the city's main shopping mall. I left him promising that I'd be there and drove straight back to the apartment and

147

made a call to Anders and a new client in Old Street. In the time between getting in and going out I flopped into the wide pool of ether emanating from my laptop screen and found a hyperlink to this in one of Petrov's many online burps:

'*Seahorses, long thought to be monogamous are in fact 'promiscuous, flighty, and more than a little bit gay' according to research published in 2007.*

'*Listening in to the sound of the silent disco at the Ballroom Extravaganza'*

'*Coffee at the Airport Lounge is best place to catch up on reading international news'*

'*The influence of pornography on sexual lifestyles has extended to the arrival of a new exhibition at Butterflies.'*

'*Business leaders forum at the Grand. Looking forward to hearing people's survival tactics.'*

'*Dinner with Francophiles at the Quartier Rouge. Rehearsing the lingua franca.'*

'*Flirting made easier by hard to get androids.'*

I was reeling by the end. How did he manage to keep up with it all? I clicked on the last tweet only to discover a parallel universe of sexually explicit messaging exchanged between Japanese social media robots masquerading as porn stars and men who convince themselves they are learning to flirt with the real thing. Petrov's conclusion? The end of civilization as we know it? Not a bit. For him it was a harbinger of things to come when artificial intelligence will provide the interactive tools for human beings to engineer their lives. I must have been browsing for over an hour before I came across these pieces and I include them here because I'd begun to notice that the information I am drawn to on the Internet is exactly as Petrov predicted. We don't stumble across it. We don't see something by accident. Every starting point is a blank field requiring words to feed it and you might think that a single thought precedes every subsequent click. But it doesn't take into account the intentions and nuances of the human heart and the darkness of the human psyche. How can any machine reader of text know what we're really searching for? Instead we are led by our daily struggle to articulate our impulses. What follows is a mixed potion of results that vaguely reflect the starting point where helpful advertising gurus and cookies attempt to clear the confusion by offering a simple set of channels to fulfilment. Still if Internet exploration is stumbling about in the dark why have I never stumbled upon an extremist Jihadist site or the sex videos of minor celebrities? Does it somehow know what I want and what I don't? I now believe that I sought this information about androids or something like it by degrees to fit my mood. It confirmed my prejudices about what I might discover later on that evening and the ever looming prospect that these men have learned automated responses to social stimuli like the herded tribes of consumers who have fallen for every successful advertising campaign in history.

That evening I showed up at the appointed hour and my first impression was that nobody had actually changed very much but they definitely weren't the same. I can't quite say what I'd been expecting but straightaway I noticed that Steve had tidied up his beard. He even looked as though he'd started to wash regularly. James had rung in the changes. Gone were the white trainers and baggy knit wear. In came pointed black shoes and tight-fitting clothes. He'd had his hair butchered by someone into something that resembled a windswept field. Neil had changed his glasses and had dropped a couple of pounds from around his waist. His face was visibly thinner. There was a smell of *eau de distinguee* about him. To my surprise they seemed quite pleased to see me.

'Back again,' said Mark, 'What's the photographer man got in store for us now? You did a great job last time by the way. I got loads more interest from women when I started using your pictures.'

'Glad it's going well. What else is new?'

'Ah,' said Steve putting his arm around me, 'That's what we're here to find out. Sharing our experiences. Did you see that I'm standing for the Greens in the local elections?'

'And you Neil? Did you end up using any of the pictures I took?'

'Mmm. I've seen better response rates to adverts for life insurance, but you can't have everything. On the positive side I've given up sugary drinks and I'm shifting some weight.'

I didn't feel comfortable. They were different, and I sensed that they were no longer talking to me in quite the same way. Something had been prompting them to improve themselves and they seemed eager to impress upon me that they were making changes to their lives. Worse still, I felt that they were expecting me to say something equally positive about myself. Of course, it had to be Capucine working in the background but can it really be that effective?

'Good evening gentlemen,' came a voice from behind us. It was Petrov. We all turned around.

'Hello. How are we all? Good. Very good. I have asked you together because I want to thank you. I want to thank you for so many things but I'm afraid I won't have time to say everything I would like. You have all given me and my team a lot of valuable insights into your lives; a second or third tier of life on top of your existing ones. Very interesting and it's taken me by surprise how quickly you have made changes. James, you even look totally different. You're in a band now?'

'Yep. I couldn't find one, so I created one. It's an electro-synth group. We haven't got a name yet. It's me and a girl called Janice. But Janice and James sounds crap. We thought about calling ourselves Nameless.'

'He hasn't got any bookings!' added Mark.

'All in good time but before we do some presentations

150

shall we head to the café first?' said Petrov.

Madame Sosostris is a bohemian café in the ramshackle old side streets of the city, behind the grand hotels and gardens of the seafront. We filed in and found a corner at the back where Petrov picked up from where he'd left off. 'I want to thank you all for your participation in what has been an incredibly useful project. You'll remember at the very beginning that I promised to share the research with you. I will still make good on that promise but what I would like to say, and I think this is of some importance, is that the results of the research are now sitting in front of your own eyes. You already know from experience what changes you have brought about. You are the living proof. So back to tonight. What have we got lined up tonight? First of all there is some prizes. Yes, I haven't forgotten.'

Petrov reached inside both pockets of his blue pin-striped jacket without any success. He checked the back pockets of his jeans. Then he seemed to pull a small envelope out of nowhere as if by sleight of hand.

'Here it is. Remember I said that for the one with the most valuable contribution on social media there would be a prize. Well, I have the result in an envelope. In true Hollywood style I can announce……that the winner is,' he said pausing to tear at the envelope with his thumb, '…….with hundreds of shares and comments on his video diaries, a fantastic ten thousand views on You Tube for his Honest Broker channel it can only be Neil. Your prize is a trip to the arena for ice-skating for two followed by a meal at the Hotel Retro. All expenses paid.'

For once Neil looked very happy with something. Petrov handed him the envelope with a voucher to claim his prize. 'Another one is for the person who has made the most important change for their own wellbeing. And that goes to Jonathan who very bravely told us about his plan to give up alcohol. He's held true to his word for six months. Not only that. His treatment is working so well that he's been

151

reunited with his children. Well done Jonathan. A trip to the Zoo for you and the kids. I'm sure they are very proud of their father. And finally, the best profile. With literally hundreds of winks, pokes, flirts and god know how many swipes there can only be one person who qualifies for this prize. It couldn't be anyone else other than Mark. You win a weekend break to Amsterdam. I hope you enjoy it. But please don't give me any credit or blame for the prizes. I didn't choose them. They were chosen by our very own Capucine who has been learning a lot about you over the last few months. She doesn't always get it right, but she is learning faster all the time.'

'Great. Thanks. The trip to Amsterdam is perfect,' said Mark, 'She got that right. But did you know that she also started monitoring my health? I kept telling her about my bad dreams and she gave me a plan to, you know, calm them down. And it worked.'

'Did she ask you for that Mark?' asked Petrov.

'Yes, she just came out with it. Are you having bad dreams? Freaky but she seemed to know and it's working. So far anyway.'

'Well gentlemen, you have been following some amazing pathways since we first began this project. Now it's time to put your research to the test. You have got to know each other quite a bit over the last few months. Hopefully you know as much as Capucine does, maybe more. So, my challenge for you is this. I've got a bag of goodies back at the university which Capucine purchased for you from the shopping mall across the road. All the products were purchased by her online. Think of them as an early Christmas present. What I would like you to do, with some of the generous research funding provided by the university, is to see if you can buy an equally appropriate or even better present for one of the members of the group. I've got an envelope for each of you with the name of the person you will be buying for. Here please take one. Inside you will also

152

have the same amount of cash we made available to Capucine. So, the only difference is what you know about the person versus what she knows. Enjoy. And I'll see you back here in a couple of hours.'

And like that they were off, disappearing into the palatial shopping mall to search for something deeply personal to the individual. I wondered if they would be swayed by advertising or special offers in a way that no machine ever would. So there we were waiting for them to return to the Madame Sosostris, an exotic paradise of bright colours and pictures of Tarot cards on the walls. I bought Petrov a cappuccino and we talked while we waited.

We talked about Tanya and Matilda. He asked me about them; what I liked about them, what I didn't. He asked me what I knew about their lives, their jobs, their education, their family lives. He asked me what I knew about how they felt, what they liked, what they hated, what they believed in. I quickly realised how little I knew and how pathetically I had been paying attention.

The men returned gradually as the evening wore on. First back was Mark.

'Easy,' he said sitting at the table next to us with his arms folded and legs spread far apart, 'It was like picking cherries. Bam, bam.'

'Is that an Ann Summers bag you've got there?' I asked.

'Yeah. He needs one of these to spice up his sex life'

'Who did you have?'

'Neil of course.'

'Ok.' said Petrov labelling the bag and sealing it at the same time, 'I'll drop it in here whilst we collect them all together. We'll mail them out to everybody next week.'

'How will I know who got me?'

'There'll be a gift tag for both.'

Neil was the next to return, smiling and sloping in with his hands in his trouser pockets.

'Did you get anything?' said Petrov.

'I tried. I looked around, but nothing inspired me. Sorry. I'll have to send it to you another time. How long did Capucine get to choose something?'

'The same amount of time. Two hours. Never mind. You're only human but if you could send something to me at the university before next week that'll be OK.'

Mark held out his hand for a high-five. Neil just smiled and nodded.

Gradually the other men came back and deposited their gifts into Petrov's bag.

'Steve,' said Mark, 'I saw you mate. Getting a manicure from those Turkish girls. What's that bag you've got? Did they manage to sell you some of their hand creams?'

'This?' Steve replied holding up the bag, 'No. I was chatting to a very nice lady in a health food shop. Sorry, I've given it away haven't I?'

'No. Not yet you haven't' said Petrov.

'Anyway, I thought you might like it,' he said handing it to Mark.

The room filled with laughter.

'Er, you needed to give that to me,' said Petrov. 'If nothing else you'll make an honest politician Steve.'

Looking back at the evening I don't think I've ever seen a group of men so happy and talkative. Petrov was in his element. He manoeuvred within the group, spending time with each man, rubbing shoulders with everyone. It was obvious, to me anyway, that this was not just a psychological experiment for him. Whatever data he was gathering in the background took a back seat last night. He cared about them, looked after them and seemed to live every moment of their experiences with them. I stayed with them the whole night, and with their permission, got out my camera to take some more shots of this band of unlikely brothers.

16.

Internet Browsing History for 20th September

8.13 Facebook - Mark Lawrence is now a friend
8.14 Facebook - Mark Lawrence photos
8.14 Facebook - Mark Lawrence photos
8.15 Facebook - Mark Lawrence photos
8.18 Account Sign-in - Cyberneticgreeneyes - Message Box
8.23 Google Search - Things to do on a first date
8.25 Top Ten First Date Ideas
8.27 Ice-skating
8.27 New cuisine
8.28 Art gallery
8.28 Aquarium
8.28 Bowling
8.30 Oprah - How Barack met Michelle and their first date

I don't need Capucine. I don't need a chatbot that directs me to the best of all possible worlds. I'm using the old methods. The floodgates holding back a sea of panic are about to crumble. I can feel the strain of expectation weighing on the soft chambers of my heart and I can feel the fear not far behind it. I looked up *ElectrikTanya* only to find her profile has gone. Has she given up on me already? I felt the need for some courage and went to the cupboard to find some Pisco and poured a small glass and knocked it back and then poured another for luck. I paced around the flat and considered going for a walk by the sea to calm down but what difference would it make? According to my browsing history it would help me to breathe properly and reduce the effects of adrenalin on my body but what does

155

the Internet really know? I dialled her number. The dialling tone droned in my ear like a clock counting down to the end of the world. She didn't pick up. I fell backwards onto the sofa with utter relief at being absolved from my fate. Then, incredibly my phone began to vibrate with an incoming call.

'Hi!' I said in a voice that didn't sound like my own.

'Hi Richard. Did you just call me?' said Tanya.

'Yes. I did. I said I would.'

'Yes,' she said.

'I've got these two tickets to go ice skating tomorrow. I wondered if you'd like to come along.'

I had no idea where all this was coming from. It didn't sound like me.

'I never skated before.'

'Are you good at falling over?'

'I can try.

'Well that's all there is to it. You can hold on to me. I'll catch you.'

I hoped that she might be smiling.

'Ok photographer man. What time?'

'Tomorrow? At six? Seven? I can pick you up from work.'

'OK, how about 6.30?'

'That's fine. 6.30. See you tomorrow.'

'Bye.'

'Bye.'

Although it was as scripted as anything I have ever said or done, I felt alive again. All my dormant hopes were revived with no thought to what might lie ahead. I hadn't intended it to be like this. I had imagined a very different kind of conversation, but it went well enough wouldn't you agree? Not my best pitch but still, it was on time and without mishap. I hadn't even bought the tickets for the skating rink. There were only a few available sessions with a skating tutor on the website last time I checked. I logged onto the site, found the last two spaces and hit the button.

The lesson was at seven. I calculated backwards from the hour I would need to arrive at the ice-rink, picking Tanya up from the museum, setting out from the flat to the hour I would have to stop work. Recollecting some of Petrov's restaurant reviews I landed on an excellent seafood place within five minutes walking distance of the ice-rink and stored the number of a taxi firm into my phone. I was done. I thought I'd unwind by re-reading *Confessions of an Advertising Man*. It's an old favourite of mine, like a comfortable pair of slippers, but I must have dozed off. I woke to the sound of a loud thump at the door.

At first I thought it must be Rosetta. When I peered through the fish-eye it was Mark standing with his face pressed close to the door. I opened it slowly.

'Mark, how's things?' I asked

'Are you busy? Can I come in?'

'What is it? I was about to go to bed to be honest.'

'Sorry mate. I don't know where else to turn. I've got to talk to someone.'

I invited him in and he went straight for the lounge, surveying the room as if he might find whatever he needed. He was panting and sweat was pouring from his face. I noticed he was fiddling with something in his combat jacket.

'Not a bad flat,' he said, 'You should have seen the way we had to look after camp in Afghanistan. It was still a crap hole though whichever way you looked at it.'

I offered to make him a drink and he asked for water. When I returned from the kitchen with a full pint glass he gulped it down in one hit.

'Yeah, sorry about this mate. I don't want to intrude on you. I messed up. Big time,' he said.

'Sit down. Just make yourself at home,' I said.

'Yeah. You know, I thought I left all that shit behind me. I thought I might have made it across you know like Nik is always saying, 'over to the other side'. But I haven't. You know the student I mentioned the other night? The blonde

157

one. I took her out tonight. It was great. We went out for drinks. We went for some tapas and she invited me back to her house. I know. I couldn't believe it. A twenty-year-old inviting me back. But then that's went it sort of went a bit weird.'

He stopped and I could see that he was fighting himself, pushing back an emotion that he didn't want to feel.

'We were going up the stairs to her room. It's in this shared student house and all that. It's a bit dirty, bit dingy. I got paranoid. I started thinking about things. Remembering things. You know. You're always watching. Feeling like you're surrounded or you're being watched. I couldn't get it out of my mind. Sorry if you haven't got a clue about what I'm talking about. I don't blame you. Why should you?'

He looked at me with disgust and then checked himself. At one stage I thought he might be about to leave. I just sat there watching him.

'Anyway. I fucked it up. I fucked the whole thing up. I can't believe it. I'm so mad at myself. I'm gonna get into a right mess now. If the police come knocking just let them in Rich. Let them come in and arrest me. I'll give myself up. I won't run. I never ran from the Taliban and I'm not gonna start running now. But before they arrive I need to tell someone what happened. I can't get her out of my head. I don't know if you can understand. I'm not making sense. I've been running. Just running. I needed to get somewhere asap. I thought about you. You won't be offended...well you're a man of the world aren't you?'

I didn't really know what to tell him. I wondered which of the neighbours had let him in. Someone leaves the door to the flats wide open.

'What happened to the girl Mark? What's her name?'

'Alicia. It's Alicia. I can't believe what I did back there? I can't believe it. I'm just playing it over and over again in my head.'

I could see that he needed time to calm down so I

158

offered to make him a proper drink, but he looked nervous about me leaving him. We just sat there for a while. Mark held his head in his hands covering his face. He seemed on the verge of collapse.

'Do you need help Mark?'

He began rubbing his face and gathered himself until he was sitting upright again.

'Don't judge me Rich. I'm not crazy. It's just the war, being discharged and all that. I must have spent a year inside a cell like this one after I left the army. A year and I didn't see a single person. I didn't go out unless it was for food. It's not good for you. Not good. I became like a hermit or something. And no-one lifted a finger to help me. No-one. It was just me, a computer and four walls. That's when I started going online and getting help from other veterans and I got in touch with people. For help. I left the flat for the first time and started to get better. I thought it might be under control now. You see I knew what Petrov was talking about in his ad. I depended on it. I'd experienced it. Talk about using the Internet to build a new life. I was already doing it. I really liked this student. Alicia. She's a nice girl. We were getting on so well and then POW. I fucked up Rich.'

'What happened?'

'We got back to the house and went through the hall and up the stairs and I started to feel down. I felt like I was on a downer all of a sudden. You know what I mean? I don't know if it was because it was so dark and the staircase was so narrow. I started to feel like I was back in those dingy farmhouses in Helmand. It felt tense. It felt like a trap. When we got into her bedroom and she turned the light straight on it was like the flash of an explosive device. Her door was still open and a big guy came out from his room to go to the loo. 'Are you OK?' he asked as if it was any of his business. I started to get jumpy. I was asking her who's that and what's he doing here and she just kept saying relax,

159

cool it, he's a housemate. I asked her if there were a lot of guys there. I meant in the house. She seemed to think I meant did she sleep with them. That's when she lost it, starting having a go at me to leave her alone, that I was a freak, an asshole. I don't know what came over me. I thought she was going to wake the whole damn house up. I tried putting my hand over her mouth to get her to stop talking for a minute and boom. It all kicked off. She screamed for help. I could hear the big guy open his door to find out what was happening. I just ran. I just had to run. I knocked the guy to the other side of the landing. She was just screaming and screaming. I ran and ran and ran. I thought the cops would have got me by now. I can't believe it man. I panicked. I just panicked. I don't know why. I'm so ashamed. So so ashamed.'

'Easy, easy,' I said. 'You're safe here. Anyone else get hurt? The girl?'

'No, like I told you. I just tried to put my hand on her mouth to shut her up, but I didn't even get close to her.'

'Don't worry. Nothing will happen. Worst case scenario is they take a statement from you. No charges. Why don't you stay until things settle down?'

I fixed him up with a strong dose of Pisco from my everlasting supply. To take his mind off things I showed him the studio at the back of the apartment.

'Nice equipment,' he said, 'It's like walking into a fridge. Everything's so white. You know I have a lot of respect for photographers. I used to know one who followed the unit. He'd been to some shit places, war zones in Africa and all that, had grenade launchers fired at him and all sorts. Been to Israel and Palestine and seen some horrific fucked up stuff over there. But that's what he loved doing. I guess you love this.'

I guided Mark to a selection of prints in the corner of the room, handing him copies of the group scenes I'd taken over the last six months. He flicked through them looking slightly puzzled. He lingered over the photos of football crowds and music festivals and became very still as if he had got lost or there was someone or something he recognized.

'I don't get it. What kind of photographer are you?' he said.

'That's a good question because I honestly haven't worked it out myself yet. I take some pictures to make a bit of money and others that are strictly for art's sake. I'm planning to do an exhibition about crowds. What do you think?'

'I don't know how you'll do it,' said Mark, 'There are some things that don't come out well in a crowd. They're not intended, or they're faked so that everyone fits in.'

I let him continue browsing on his own and went into the lounge to straighten a few things out, checking the time and looking out of the window for any signs of the police. There was very little I could see in the darkness and the rain.

'Mark, you're welcome to stay here tonight on the couch but do you mind if I do some work?'

'No, that's fine mate. I didn't mean to tread on your toes. Yeah. I'll leave you to it. Can I ask you a question? Are you part of the research? Is Petrov monitoring your laptop like the rest of us?'

'Not as far as I know,' I said.

'Well, do you mind if I watch some TV?'

He switched on the set and stretched out on the couch. I watched him occasionally from the dining table where I resumed the old mission of reprogramming myself to become reasonably attractive to the opposite sex. From time to time I thought I heard him dozing off and as we crept towards the early hours of the morning I took the remote from beside his still hand and switched off the screen. He stayed sound asleep. I got a blanket from the airing cupboard and covered him slowly taking care not to make any sudden movements. I don't need Capucine. I know who I am and what I want. Does Mark? Are we friends or is this

161

what being friended means?

12.18 YouTube - PTSD - awareness video
12.23 YouTube - My life with PTSD - US Vets
12.42 YouTube - How to help someone with PTSD
12.59 YouTube - How to be natural on a date - The Guardian
01.14 YouTube - Ice Skating for Beginners - How to lace up your skates
01.18 YouTube - How to Ice skate: the Push Off
01.23 YouTube - How to Ice skate: the Turn

17.

When I woke up the next day, Mark had gone but he'd left me a note

I got up early. Thanks for the chat. I hope you don't mind but I made myself some breakfast. See you around buddy.

But I don't want to talk about that. I'm sure he'll be OK. He will be OK won't he? I'll look him up on social media later. Something else has happened that has taken me away from all that. What I would give to be a photographer with a photographic memory. I arrived at the museum to meet Tanya exactly to the minute; no sooner, no later. She was already waiting for me. How different from Matilda I remember thinking. As soon as she saw me she greeted me with a wave, a wide smile and a kiss on both cheeks.

'I am so exciting. I never skated before,' she said, 'Have you?'

'Yes,' I said, 'Once or twice. But that was ages ago.'

'It's fun no?'

'Of course. The class is starting soon. We need to get our skates on.'

'Yes, you are right. Do they borrow you the skates when we get there?'

It was a warm evening in September. The sun was beginning to dip towards the horizon and there was a sense of carelessness about everything as if the summer was still there to be enjoyed one last time. The skating rink was heaving with people. Tanya was struggling with lacing up her skates. She'd got cramp as she tried to squeeze her foot in. I knelt down to rub the base of her foot to try to alleviate the pain and it seemed to do the trick.

'You know how to massage?' she asked as she opened

her eyes.

'No, I'm just making it up as I go along,' I said.

She looked at me quizzically as if she wasn't sure whether this was all part of the self-deprecation which makes up a typical Englishman's character.

'It's very good.'

'Better?' I asked.

She nodded.

'OK, let's get these skates on. I'll loosen these laces a bit. They're all a bit skew whiff.'

'Sku what?'

'It's an English phrase. You know. Skew whiff. It's all a bit out of line. Not straight.'

'Sku weave? I never heard of that before,' she giggled, 'Sku weave?'

'Do you have those kinds of phrases in Spanish?'

'Yes, but not like these funny English words. How am I to know English if I don't know words like Sku weave? So it means….not straight. So why don't you just say not straight.'

'Because,' I said helping her into the other skating boot, 'because, we like words to stand in for other words. It means you don't have to say the same old things over and over again. And as we're in an ice-skating rink this is the perfect place to practice it. You can say, 'Richard. I think your skating is very sku weave.'

We took to the ice. How can I describe it? I want to be able to remember this again, almost exactly as it was. We took to the ice like children and waited for our tutor to arrive. Tanya was still laughing about my strange vocabulary. I was intrigued by how easily she seemed to be able to enjoy herself. I took her hand in mine as I stepped tentatively onto the ice and she followed. She looked at me as if to say, 'Now what?' and we began by slowly inching our feet ahead, almost as if we were hoping that by respecting the ice it might go easy on us. I suggested that we form a train and

164

that she get behind me and hold onto my waist but as I tried to make some headway on the ice I fell flat on my knees before her like a poor man's Lancelot. She laughed as I scrambled to get back up. I held out a hand for her to help me but as soon as she pulled her grip loosened and she tumbled straight onto her backside.

'You do that on purpose!' she cried, 'Help me up. Please!'

'No, no. I'm not falling for the same trick.'

We were still close enough to the barriers to pull ourselves up. I clambered to my feet first and helped Tanya to hers and it was then that I saw the gliding presence of an elegant woman whooshing past and calling everyone together into the centre of the ice-rink. The lesson was about to begin.

Tanya gripped my waist and we started off on a journey to the centre of the ice rink, struggling like hatchlings. We shuffled our way around the edges at first, clinging on for safety. Younger and more experienced skaters who had long since adapted themselves to the ice swooped past, putting us to shame with displays of speed and balance. Looking up at the passing skaters I noticed Sabrina. She clocked me and nodded very slightly before gliding away like a ballerina followed by a man who was like a dog scampering after its owner. It was Neil. He passed me by without making eye contact. I sensed it was deliberate and remembering how to push off I guided Tanya to a semi-circle which had formed around the tutor.

'Good evening everyone. My name is Karla,' she said,' I am from Norway. I will be teaching you some simple beginners steps this evening to help you to become more confident skaters. Don't worry if this is your first time, we won't be forcing you to do bunny hops from day one. We will be focusing on turning and keeping balance on the ice."

And so our lesson began with this young Scandinavian beauty whose bodily strength and poise kept her audience captivated. After a lot of knee bending and leaning on our partners, she got us learning to glide forwards in a straight line. She kept couples together and paired up anyone who had come to the lesson alone. Was that why Neil had turned up? Was that what Capucine had intended to happen all along? Then, when she had finished a couple of simple exercises, she sent us on our way to practice. Tanya and I pushed off and we were cut loose from the group. I started to grow in confidence, skating at increasing speed and although I could remember how to turn, I just couldn't do it quickly enough. My legs wouldn't get going and the hoardings at the far end of the rink loomed like buffers at the end of a railway. I hit them head on, my knees slamming into the padding. Tanya took the soft option of running straight into my back, squashing my cock against the railings and nearly tipping me over.

'Gotcha!' she cried, 'Now don't move.'

'How can I move? I think I might be impaled on something.'

'Wait. I'm going to fall. Don't move.'

'I need you to move first. I think you've got me in an arm lock.'

'Don't move! AAAAAHHHHHHHHHHHHH!'

And she was down.

'Don't laugh at me mister!'

We tried to copy some of Karla's moves, skating around, holding onto each other until we were stable enough to let go. We were equally matched, equally hopeless. I don't think I've laughed so much in a very long time. I can't remember feeling so comfortable in my own incompetence. Tanya seemed to be enjoying it. She pulled so many strange and contorted faces as she tried to keep going; worried frowns, mouth wide open with fear, lips pouting with concentrated effort and little dances of joy as she shrugged her shoulders and bobbed her head along to the music booming out across the stadium.

I hadn't thought it was possible to feel like this. I loved it. I loved seeing her laugh and smile. I thought I'd lost all feelings when I lost my former life. As I look back over the previous pages I can't quite imagine what it was like. It's strange isn't it? Waiting for the future to be different, wondering if the present will go on forever, trying to shed the past. We think we're the same but we're not. We're just not suited to measuring our feelings over time. They get lost as they recede into the past. We forget. And Neil? I completely forgot about him. We saw him skating forwards and falling, getting up and starting all over again just like the rest of us. He had paired up with Sabrina, but she had easily surpassed him and was busy doing her own circuits of the rink; backwards, forwards and in little circles.

We left the ice rink a little battered and bruised. As we slipped away from the car park I could feel the weight of her body leaning against mine as if she hadn't registered that we had moved from ice to tarmac.

'What shall we do now?' she said.

'Are you hungry? Do you like seafood?'

I already knew from her profile that it was one of her favourites. So off we went to Petrov's favourite seafood restaurant. I half expected to find him there as I pushed open the doors. Inside a waiter showed us to a small table in a quiet and intimate part of the restaurant. In all the months I've been living in this city I've never bothered to eat out. In the candlelight Tanya looked more beautiful than ever. Her dark brown eyes seemed to turn black in the flickering light and her smile made everything she did appear charming and indulgent, from fiddling with the rings on her fingers to propping her head up with the front of her hand. You see, although I know this is all a trick of the romantic imagination, I was glad to feel it returning. I knew where this script was going but instead of feeling like a failed actor lunging at any part I felt as though this particular part had been written specifically with my character in mind.

And we just talked. She asked me about my family, my childhood, my life. She wanted me to describe things, tell her about things. It didn't matter what it was. As a fellow artist I imagined she was trying to draw up a portrait of her subject. I asked about her. She told me that she was the chubby kid with glasses who always had her hand up in class. Her two closest friends were her dog Nero and a boy named Antonio who she used to play with in front of their apartment block. Her father paid for her to go to art school by taking on an extra job. She found the details of my life funny.

'Your father made money from toilet paper?' she kept repeating much to her own disbelief.

'*Same shit different day* was his motto.'

I write this only twenty-four hours after the event. Have I captured the essence of our meeting? I want to remember the situations, the strange concoction of tastes, smells, appearances and feelings before it's too late. Soon, I will only remember one or two moments. What did we eat? We shared a house platter of lobster, crab, moules marinieres, Greenland prawns, rock oysters and cockles with several glasses of wine. You see how it goes? I can still taste the combination of flavours. This is where you can probably insert your own script, the one that brought you together with someone you still care about. She liked crab best. I preferred the lobster.

I said, 'You know it's not too late to look at some of my work.'

'When?'

'Tonight.'

She smiled.

'I was meaning to ask you something?' she said. 'Why did you put a funny picture in place of your real one? I mean on the website.'

'Why?'

'Yes.'

'Because I didn't really believe in any of the profiles. They all looked fake. So I thought if I make mine look deliberately fake it will have the opposite effect. I thought it might send a signal out to the world about my sense of humour.'

'Me too. That's what I did. I could tell as soon as I looked at yours that you were thinking of the same thing. That's why I sent you a message.'

'And I have to say I much prefer you to the dog.'

'It didn't put you off?' she asked.

'No, it made me more curious.'

'It worked then. You came looking. It's a pity I have to go back.'

'Perhaps there's still time to persuade you to stay.'

'Maybe. Can you order a taxi?'

I got the restaurant to call a cab. We waited outside and laughed about the unfortunate Neil and his clumsy attempts to keep up with a twenty-year-old woman. A cold wind was blowing in from the sea and we huddled close to one another.

'And you,' she said, 'You said you could skate and you couldn't.'

'I had a few lessons once. I sort of got dragged along to do them.'

She smiled again, and I leaned in to kiss her. She pulled me closer and put her arms around my neck. When I pulled away we stood face to face holding each other's finger tips just as we had on the ice rink.

When the taxi arrived I gave the driver my address. The journey home, the laughter on the stairs, the fumbling to get the key into the lock of the apartment door. Do I need to commit any more to paper? My father always used to say that one of the essential characteristics of a decent life is discretion.

18.

Internet Browsing History for 23rd September

10.03 Heathrow: Heathrow Departures - Live Updates
10.05 Heathrow:Heathrow: Scheduled Departures 9 Oct
10.14 Facebook - Tanya Lopez
10.15 Facebook - Tanya Lopez
10.16 Facebook - Mark Lawrence
10.17 Facebook - Matilda Johnson
10.18 Finding a Job in Madrid: Getting Started:Expatica Spain
10.24 Trabajo InfoJobs
10.27 Working in Spain: A Guide for English Speakers
10.29 JobSearch Results: Linkedin
10.30 Campaign Manager - Madrid: Linkedin

So, what do I do? Since she's going back to Spain a week on Friday should I conclude that this is it? It could be over just as soon as it began. I could visit Madrid every couple of weeks or every month but is that enough? It doesn't feel enough. I've only just got going as a freelance photographer. I want this relationship to go on but I'm not sure how determined she is to go home. Could she find some more work with another museum? There must be a position available in London somewhere? I could help her but then I can only just support myself. What use am I likely to be if she gets stuck here? We could cope but is coping any kind of life? My mind is in a mess. There is so much to do. I've been offered an assignment in the Alps and there's a small but demanding string of enquiries about my availability for a series of professional portraits next week. Where did they come from? They came from my very own design; a mixture of the new website and having good contacts. For once I wish people wouldn't put in a good word for me.

16.06 BBC Languages - Learn Spanish
16.08 BBC Languages - Spanish for Beginners
16.10 BBC Languages - Talking About Your Family
16.16 BBC Languages - Talking About Work
16.19 BBC Languages - Introductions
16.23 Rapido UK - Find a Spanish Teacher
16.25 Rapido UK - Online Tutors - Maria Jose
16.31 Rapido UK - Find an English Teacher
16.35 Inbox - New Message - Tanya Lopez

Como hablar espanol rapidamente? I have no chance of being able to pass myself off as an intermediate to fluent speaker any time soon. I would need a tutor. Would that be enough? It would still take too long. Fear and necessity are the vital ingredients if I am to have a chance of learning anything that doesn't come naturally to me. Perhaps I could learn Spanish off the cuff and under duress in Spain. Quiero un café con leche? Y tu? La pena de muerte? I got a message from Tanya earlier today. She asked if I could meet her for a coffee. I suggested the Madame Sosostris. If only the famous clairvoyant could predict how this is all going to end. Things are moving quickly now. I may have to be brief.

19.

.

24th September

I offered to help her get to the airport. I said I'd drive her there on Friday morning and help her with her luggage. I can't believe what a chivalrous android I'm turning into. Let me recap. I have just offered to help the one woman I really care about to disappear from my life as quickly as she entered it. It's like I'm assisting in my own downfall. I toyed with the idea of surprising her by buying a one-way ticket for myself. It's possible. There are still some tickets left. Then again, isn't this a bit too possessive? Men and women constantly meet and part all the time and nothing like a permanent arrangement is implied. I am already jealous of her relationship with her home country. I almost collapsed with relief when we met today. She still looks pleased to see me. As soon as we sat down I knew it wasn't going to be one of those sombre conversations; one of those encounters where a lot of effort and coffee is expended on procrastinating about saying the relationship will never work.

No, she was delightful and full of energy. We talked about what we'd been up to in the hours since we last met. The most trivial things became of immense interest.

'It's such a shame you're going,' I said.

'Yes, it's a pity,' she said, 'But I may come back if I can find some more work. I need to get back to my studio as well and to continue with my art. It's all waiting for me. Like a family.'

If only my rival was another man. He could be contested but an artist and her art? Never.

'I need to get back to work,' she went on 'creating some

new pieces.'

And that's exactly what I would have expected her to say. What right had I to take her away from her passion? Or her country? I mentioned the new assignment in Switzerland and that I would need to get busy with arranging my own exhibition.

'Oh, you should. You must do it. Why don't you start with one of the art festivals? I will arrange for someone to give you some wall space in the autumn festival.'

I can tell by the look in her eye that it's a done deal. It led very naturally on to the subject of her going away party. Everyone will be there including all the friends she made at the gallery and her network of *émigrés* from across the city. I need to be brief. I haven't got as much time on my hands. I am about to head back to her place for a meal.

25th September

I don't know where to begin. We passed the rest of the evening together and it was as good an evening as I've ever enjoyed. We collapsed on the sofa and spent the rest of the night watching a film. She fell asleep on my chest and as I started to drift off to sleep I was woken by the vibrations of the phone in my pocket. Tanya woke up immediately.

'Check it,' insisted Tanya, 'It could be important.'

I took the phone from my jeans. It was a missed call from Mark. Seconds later I got a text from him.

hi rich, bad, bad news. neil is dead. can't believe it. call me when you get this.

I called him back straight away. He was surprisingly calm.

'I could have told him he was going about things the wrong way. He just wouldn't listen. You could see it coming. He kept saying he would die alone. He wouldn't talk to people. It's what happens to people when they don't get the support. They just go down and down. It was just one more tragedy waiting to happen. Did you see he'd posted the same message, *'See you on the other side'* in a number of different places?'

'That was Petrov's phrase,' I said.

'Yeah, I know. But you know as well as I do that it doesn't mean that,' said Mark, ' I messaged back that things must be going well. Nothing. He's only gone and topped himself hasn't he?'

'How did you find out?'

'Steve. They'd become good friends. They were supposed to be going on a fishing trip this weekend. Steve couldn't get hold of him. He kept calling him up but there was no answer. Eventually he went round his house. His wife answered the door and told him. She's devastated.'

'Wife?'

'Yeah, I know, wife and three kids. Who knew about that? He must have been making tracks to get out.'

Then Mark said he had to go. He was getting another text coming through. Tanya had been biting her nails and pacing up and down the room. Occasionally she tried to say something but stepped back.

'Are you ok?' I asked Mark.

'Me? I'm Ok. It's a stab in the guts but I'll be fine.'

'Who else knows about this?'

'I've been in touch with more or less everyone. I've been trying you all day.'

'Petrov?' I asked.

'Nik?' he said, 'Yeah. He knows.'

'How did he take it?'

'He went very quiet. Very quiet. He was thinking, taking it all in I suppose. I almost hung up on him. If it wasn't for the fact that I've seen shock before he took the news like a man.'

'Do you know anything more? Cause of death?'

'Nothing too specific yet but it looks like suicide. Pills probably. A few of us want to go to the funeral. Steve's trying to find out. Sorry if I ruined your evening.'

With that he hung up and I looked at Tanya. She knew it was bad. I got her to sit down and told her what had happened. Tears sprang to her eyes. It was like returning to the land of 'No-Hope', to those strange and hyper-real days following Helen's betrayal. Tanya had seen him stumbling around on the ice for only a fraction of time and even that was enough to affect her. I held Tanya in my arms and gave her a long hug, but I could feel the same numbing of emotion flowing back through my body like the injection of a drug. We stayed up talking about him. We went through what we realised was his false social media account. It contained a least two years of history. He'd posted the photographs I'd taken of him with a seagull lurking at his shoulder. There was another of him smiling with his arms around James and Steve and a particularly suave one of him in an open neck shirt, smiling for the camera which he'd saved as his main profile picture. Judging by the angle and distance I guessed this was one he'd taken himself. He had a small collection of eighty or so friends and unlike the man I met in person he shared and posted relentlessly; jokes, amusing videos, wry updates on the so-called lavish lifestyle of a high-flying broker. There was no mention of his children or wife.

'What do you think? Did this girl at the ice-rink have anything to do with it?' asked Tanya, 'I could tell he was unhappy when you pointed him out to me. Running after that girl. He looked like a ridiculous old man.'

'I doubt he was involved with her. I mean I don't know. But do you think they actually went on a date together? It didn't look like it to me.'

No, and no matter how long we browsed his mythical profile and his equally illusory photos neither of us could truly understand it, unless this was merely the embryo for a new life which had failed to grow. Had he given up all hope of making it to the alternative life he'd envisioned? Was it a strategic decision that it was better to accept no life than fail to live the one he wanted?

'Are you going to be OK?' asked Tanya, 'I feel bad about leaving you.'

'Don't worry. I think I should stay here for a while. I didn't know him very well, but I feel that I ought to be around. Even if it's just to pay my respects with the other men from Petrov's group, I feel as though I owe it to them. My photography helped him to shape that online profile.'

'But it's not your fault. How could you know?'

It's true I hardly knew Neil, but his digital identity had left its mark and I felt strangely drawn to him, recognizing the sheer struggle involved in attempting to break out and start a new life.

'Look at him there. In that one. I didn't take that one.' He was pictured with a crumpled but proud man on one side and a white haired and refined looking woman in a hat on the other. Both had their arms around him. In the centre sporting a black gown and mortar board Neil looked no younger than the middle-aged man he would go on to become. He must have been proud of his life once.

20.

We experience time very differently in the online world. There appears to be a dual system in operation where time in the digital world and the real world, although working to the same clock, travels at quite different speeds. The digital world has a lot in common with dreaming where the brain can seemingly compress all kinds of possible outcomes from the most everyday social interactions into a few fleeting moments. If it happens to you whilst you're driving a car or walking somewhere it can often make you feel as though you've simply jumped ahead in the journey without being conscious of all the tarmac, trees and houses that have passed by in the interim. Sitting in front of a screen is like that. One thing leads to another; the flow of human emotions, all its lusts, curiosities, intrigues, ambitions, worries, catharses carry you on with their own momentum. Sometimes I see my browsing history as something sequential rather like a novel but more often it appears to be a form of grasping for expression from the brain's automatically evolving operating system. One thing you can be sure of is that the digital clock in the corner of your screen is timing your capacity for evolution. But it's not just the perception of time. It's the compression of time that's impressive. If misunderstandings and rumour can easily erupt from gossip in a small group of people how much more misinformation and even downright mendacity can occur in a world where a thought can quickly become the written word and where the written word can be broadcast to millions of people, all within a matter of several seconds. This is how things seem to be happening now. Petrov is in trouble. Sabrina too.

It was Friday morning and I'd been getting ready to take Tanya to the airport. The car had been parked outside the flat for a while and I promised myself I'd check it over, so I got up quite early and went out to start her up and see if everything was okay. As I leaned over the engine to check the oil I heard the sound of footsteps walking at pace behind me. Before I could turn I saw a hand reach out and the bonnet of the car come down hard, hitting the back of my skull. At first I thought it was a prank by some kids but as I tried to get up I felt my arms being restrained and my face pushed down onto the engine. Slowly the bonnet was raised again. I saw a man; his shaven hair and pasty complexion, the look of a dog, with a powerful jaw, the calm smirk on his face. It was Sabrina's stalker, the foreign postman, the man I'd photographed outside the flat. He'd come back as he'd promised he would. I could just about make out another man. All I could see was a beard and his belly pushing into me as he held me down.

'Nice car,' said the postman, 'We help you to fix it?'

'No thanks'.

He leaned in to my face until I could smell the mixture of gum and cigarettes on his breath. Then he brought out a knife and pointed it somewhere between my eyes. It was all a blur.

'You take us to the flat now,' he said, 'Don't be stupid and we leave you alone. Come.'

The bearded man hoisted me up and we marched to the flats. As we arrived at the front door the postman reached into my pockets and pulled out my set of keys. Within seconds he had opened the front door and we were inside, standing in the main hallway. As soon as the door had closed I was certain I was about to meet a grisly end but I couldn't accept that my time was up. I should have been more afraid, ready to fight for my life but I felt frozen, hoping that an opportunity to escape might present itself. I thought of Tanya. I thought of her face and couldn't believe for a second that I might never see her again. As we approached the stairs the postman spoke to me very quietly, never taking his eyes off mine for a second.

'Now, you take us to the door of the girls. You knock and wait for it to open. That's it. You say your name and that's it. Anything stupid and we kill you.'

He waved his blade in my face again and we made our way up the staircase until I was in front of the door. I prayed that Rosetta was not in but as soon as I knocked I heard her familiar sing-song voice. As soon as she heard me reply I could hear her feet scuttling to the door. She can't have checked before she opened it, but she knew what was happening as soon as she saw the men. Too late. The postman grabbed her and pushed one hand around her mouth. With one arm behind my back and another clasping the back of my neck the bearded one shoved me into the flat and then down onto the floor keeping my head still with his boot.

'Leave him, please,' pleaded Rosetta as the man briefly relinquished his grip on her face and she was bundled into one of the bedrooms. She re-emerged and was forced into each room until he could be certain there was no-one else in the flat. Then he took her into one of the rooms and closed the door behind him. All I could do was wait. The flat was silent. Nothing happened for several interminable minutes until I heard the sound of Rosetta babbling endlessly in words I couldn't understand. Then the door to the bedroom was opened again. I listened out for Rosetta but could hear nothing. A pair of boots appeared before my face. I was brought to my feet again. The postman had a phone in his hand which he slipped into his jacket pocket.

'Now you,' he said.

He grabbed me hard behind one my ears and reeling with pain I followed them as they dragged me next door. They took my keys and let themselves in.

'Camera. Give it.'

I nodded to the coffee table in the corner. He gathered the Nikon up in his grubby hands, manhandling it until he had figured out how to remove the chip. Then he placed it on the windowsill and opened up the window.

'What a pity,' he said.

Within seconds he had nudged it slightly and it was gone, crashing onto the pavement below.

'Next time be more careful.'

And to my surprise they just left. They disappeared in a hurry down the stairs and were gone. I picked myself up and began to stagger outside but Rosetta was already on her way to see me.

'They want Sabrina,' she said, as she burst into the room, 'Do something. They will kidnap her. They'll kill her.'

'What did you tell them?'

'I had to tell them where she is. I had to tell him otherwise he was going to kill me. She's now living at a house on Critchley Road. Near the university. I had to tell him, and he wanted to know where she is. At the university I said but he knew that. He kept saying 'Where? Where?' Oh god forgive me. I told him everything. They left me this.'

She waved a phone in front of me.

'Why?'

'I don't know. They took mine and he gave me his.'

I don't know how he could have figured it out but perhaps through a series of near misses he realised his phone was giving his location away. Sabrina hadn't much time. I sent Tanya a text to let her know I was on my way and called Petrov. I felt sure he might be able to do something. Rosetta paced up and down the flat crossing herself and kissing the crucifix she wore around her neck. Petrov didn't answer.

'Do you want me to call the police? Ambulance?'

Rosetta shook her head, 'No. Please don't. I'm alright. I don't want to be any trouble. You go and find her before they get her.'

I sent Petrov a message to warn him of what was heading Sabrina's way. I called the university switchboard and tried to explain to the receptionist that one of their students was in danger but somehow my words got tangled.

'I want to speak to someone in security. There's a student who's being stalked. He's heading to the campus.'

'Could you give me a name sir?'

'Sabrina.'

'Sabrina who? I'm sorry but you're going to have to give me her surname?'

Rosetta shook her finger at me. 'She's Anna. Anna Mihajlovic.'

'Anna,' I said, 'Her name is Anna Mihajlovic. There can't be more than one. Can you not look it up in your records?'

She must have taken me for a crank and hung up.

'She told me about this boyfriend,' said Rosetta, 'She was telling me to watch out for him. That's why she moved here. He didn't want her to come to England.'

My laptop was still open and so I flicked through an exchange of tweets from Petrov to the rest of the research group; first Mark then Neil. Did Petrov connect with her? They were linked. I clicked into her profile and hovered over the 'Message' button. It let me through and I began to type.

anna, it's rosetta. your ex-bf came to the flat. They are on their way to find you at the house, sorry. let us know you are ok.

We waited. I paced around the flat, worried about Anna and Tanya, while Rosetta stood watching the screen on my laptop.

'She replied! Come quickly,' blurted out Rosetta.

Call me x

I dialled her on my landline and put her on speakerphone.

'Hello?' she answered.

'Anna! Are you ok?' yelled Rosetta.

'Please, I'm fine. Don't worry. He has been following me

everywhere. I hope you are OK? Did he hurt you?'

'Oh my God. I thought they were going to kill us, but we are thankfully OK. All OK. I worry about you my dear.'

'I'm afraid I have some bad news,' I said, 'He left his telephone here so you won't be able to track his movements.'

There was silence and then, 'The police will pick them up. Don't worry about me. I must go. Sorry.'

'Look after yourself. Watch your back.'

By now I was running late; an hour late. I left the flat and promised to check on Rosetta when I returned. I drove like a madman, careering around the city like a clown, jumping a red light in order to get to Tanya. When I pulled up outside her flat she was already closing the front door and turning the key. I apologised and rushed over to help her with her cases.

'No, you take that one,' she said pointing to the heavier of the two.

I carried it across the road while she trundled behind me to the car. We packed them both into the boot without speaking.

'Are you looking forward to seeing your family?' I asked as we buckled up.

'Mmmm,' she replied.

'I'm sorry I was late. You wouldn't believe what just happened.'

'It's ok.'

'Have you got someone to pick you up when you get to Madrid?'

'Yes,' she said.

It was like that for at least five or ten minutes. The machine response, the robot in me began to surface again. I had infused myself with doses of Petrov's online lectures over the past few months and they began to act as a kind of antidote. I could sense him reprimanding me for being so coy. She needed to know the truth so I began to tell Tanya what had happened. She listened intently as if I might be fishing from an inexhaustible stock of creative excuses from my days in advertising and just nodded and looked straight ahead.

'Are you ok? You have some marks on the back of your neck.'

'Handprints?' I asked.

She smiled.

'I don't know if I'm OK. I haven't had a minute to think it about it yet. I was worried about you.'

'You should see someone. You must be in shock.'

'I'm getting used to shock I think. I'll be OK.'

Now she's gone I can easily convince myself that I see things more clearly. I can see the possibility of a new life. I can look back and see the strain of choosing between two lives, running in parallel to one another. As we sped towards the airport and the motorway began to separate it felt as though we were being forced to take a road where we were inevitably going to cut ourselves off from one another forever. We parked at the terminal and I helped Tanya with her bags. She smiled empathetically as she watched me struggle to take her monumental luggage out of the car. I walked behind her all the way to the check-in desk, following her quick strides as she searched the terminal's departure boards and moved off quickly, turning occasionally to check that I was still there. Once the luggage had been weighed and labelled I suggested that we get a coffee so we sat down in a café to wait. I wanted to stop what was happening. I wanted to put the clock back a couple of days so that we could enjoy one another again. She had stepped onto the dreadful treadmill of international travel and its tortuous process of departure. All I could think about were ways to suspend it or even reverse it so that we could put her suitcase back in the car and drive home.

Then she asked me, 'Are you Ok?'

'Yes,' I said, 'Well, no, not really.'

'Me too,' she said. 'I prefer not to go. But you know I have to.'

'I know' I said, 'I'll come out and visit you very soon.'

'Don't be sad Richard. It's not the end of the world. I'm only two hours away. I'll show you the city and you can meet my family.'

I haven't spoken to anyone in my own family for nearly a month. Tanya rings somebody in her family circle at least once a day. I finished my coffee long before she'd even got half way through hers. She must have sensed that it was the right time to leave and began to gather up her hand luggage.

'I think I should go. There's a big line for security now. I've got a bottle of water. Here you better have it,' she said.

I took the bottle and we walked side by side to the barriers stretching from wall to wall with its giant snake of people awaiting the security monitors. She turned around to face me.

'Have a good trip,' I said. I leaned in to kiss her and she threw her arms around my neck, pulling me into her. We held on like pair of entwined seahorses and I can't be sure who pulled away first. All I can remember now is the look of tenderness in her eyes and her smiling face. She turned and shrugged her shoulders as if to apologise. Then she took out her boarding pass and waved it at me cheerily as she waited in line for her turn to pass through the sliding doors that opened onto the next zone. I lost sight of her for a few minutes as she walked underneath the metal detectors and was swamped by other people picking up their things on the other side. That was it. Goodbye. I never saw her after that. I walked back to the car. Before I could even turn the key in the ignition I could feel myself beginning to break down. The pain was too great. I felt tears running down my cheeks and tried to push them back up my face to where they should remain. This woman had chosen to spend her last few days in England with me and had left an imprint I hadn't expected. Any recollection of the happiness we had experienced together only served to drive open an even bigger wedge between this life and the one that has just been lost. I may have been crying for my old love, Helen and what had happened to us. I cried for Neil and the despair he must have felt over his own love. It was a mess. The whole thing is a bloody mess of crossed wires and connections. After a while I dabbed my face with my sleeves and sat upright gazing out at the rows of parked cars in front of me. I drove home in silence and checked on Rosetta. She was out. When I fished for my phone I saw that I'd received a couple of new messages. One was from Tanya; *getting on the plane now. speak to you soon darling xxxx.*. The other was a message notifying me of several missed calls from Petrov.

21.

Internet Browsing History 1st October

13.12 Twitter

13.13 Nikola Petrov (npetrov70) on Twitter

13.14 Twitter/npetrov 70: That's not really fair comment...

13.14 Twitter/npetrov 70: It's not for me to say...

13.18 Twitter/yummynikki : you ruined our lives...

13.18 Twitter/catlovingqueen: people like you make me sick...

13.18 Twitter/yummynikki: the mask is off now - FAKE...

13.18 Twitter/catlovingqueen: all these academics are the same #selfish

13.20 Twitter/babybunny: mysogynist...

13.59 Facebook - log in

13.59 Facebook - Anna Mihajlovic

13.59 Facebook - Tanya Lopez/pictures

14.00. Facebook - Tanya Lopez/pictures

14.00 Facebook - Tanya Lopez/pictures

14.00 Facebook - Tanya Lopez/pictures

14.02 Skype - Login

14.03 Apartmentsforhire - Spain - Madrid - Luxury apartments

14.04 RentalMadrid - One bedroom apartments

14.05 RentalMadrid - Where to stay in Madrid

14.10 Google Search - How to make long distance relationships work 10 tips

14.16 Long distance relationships - How to survive them

14.19 Long distance relationships - waking up next to your laptop and other

14.26 Hotmail - Login

14.26 Hotmail - Inbox

14.27 Hotmail - Sent Items

14.28 YouTube
14.53 Facebook - new message - Mark Lawrence
14.56 Facebook - new message - Mark Lawrence
14.59 Blogger - The Natural Man - Nikola Petrov
15.00 Google Search - The Natural Man
15.01 Scriptorium - What the Bible says of Natural Man
15.04 Who is the Natural Man in 1 Corinthians?
15.03 Wikipedia - Jean-Jacques Rousseau

I've been at a loose end. I tried Petrov several times, but he hasn't been picking up. Sabrina/Anna's whereabouts is still uncertain. I searched for any online activity on her account but there were no updates to her status or any clues as to what had happened to her from her recent activity; just a picture of her out with the girls drinking cocktails. Petrov though, had been busy. The women were after him. A hail of commentators had begun attacking him on his Twitter feed, accusing him of running a school for extra-marital affairs. One of them held him responsible for the sexual exploitation of women, another accused him of sponsoring rape culture. The most poignant exchanges were from someone I guessed was Neil's wife. She raged with despair at the devastation she believed Petrov had brought into their lives. I pitied him. He was being swept away by a storm. Reading through the replies I followed his unfailingly polite attempts at explanation but each one was met with a formidable counter-blast. No-one else appeared to be coming to his aid but then why would anyone risk facing the wrath of the righteous mob?

The sound of a key being inserted into a lock next door brought me back to the real world. I listened out for Rosetta and could hear her opening and closing kitchen cupboards through the thin walls. She was safe at least. I went out and knocked on her door. I could feel her presence behind the door as she inspected me through the spy-hole.

'Richard. Are you alone?'

'Yes,' I said, 'There's no-one else here.'

'Sorry my love but I'm too scared to open the door now. After what happened.'

'Don't worry. If you can give me your number we can speak over the phone.'

She went away and then came back, posting a scrap of paper with her number on it underneath the door. I went back to the flat and dialled her from my laptop. She was apologetic about everything.

'This is the first and last time anything like that has ever happened to me. I am moving out.'

'And Anna? Do you know how she is?'

'She's safe', she said, 'thank God she's in safe hands. The university are giving her an escort to the campus each day. I gave Anna his phone so maybe they will track them down. But who will protect her at night or when they are not watching?'

'Is he still at large?'

'Yes, if only I'd bought a camera for the door. None of this would have happened. I feel like I've lost a friend.'

'What are you going to do now?'

'I used to live in a quiet area,' she said, 'Maybe I'll go back to that.'

Perhaps Caspian has a solution that will protect her. I hope so. With that we ended our chat and I returned to the news feeds about Petrov. Speculation was rife about a young blonde he'd been seen with at the university. It wasn't long before the word 'exploitation' was mentioned. Petrov himself had gone quiet and I suspected he probably knew that nothing he could say would placate the one-eyed internet informers and their determination to silence him but the temptation to enter the fray was overwhelming. I pitied him, knowing, as I did that what he wanted was for people to be able to make an informed choice about life rather than feel obliged to accept whatever they were presented with. There is always a hope behind a desire and not far away from hope is the scent of utopia. I began to tweet as if I'd dropped by, a casual eavesdropper on a café conversation;

Has anyone read his blog?…

just read a few and can't find anything about infidelity or secrecy

found a whole article on women protecting themselves through new AI devices though…

What would you suggest? Censorship? Ritual beheading?

It was useless. They saw me for what they wanted me to be, a male trying desperately to justify male hopes and desires, and ultimately an apologist for all their consequences by default. I think my intervention encouraged two others to join in on Petrov's side. She gave herself the title of *herspace93* although it wasn't lost on me that this might have been an elaborate double-bluff.

'commenting on something you haven't read makes you an abuser of information' was *herspace93*'s opening riposte.

Then Mark joined the fray, *'too right. I worked with the guy. He saved my life. Couldn't save everyones ☹'*

In this curious battle of troll against troll it was difficult to find any sense in the volley of ad hominem remarks that cascaded down the screen. The battle raged on and my thoughts turned to Petrov again. Had he been experimenting on me? I wondered if his consent to being profiled in a creative magazine had not in fact been orchestrated by him to encourage me to register on his website; to put myself in the hands of Capucine. Was that what he was doing? I think he saw the advertising background in my career and had a role for me in mind; a mix of both observer and engineer. What harm had it done? Neil had committed suicide, but I can't see how that can be laid at Petrov's feet. And the other men? I don't know. Before Petrov I'd met Matilda and stalled. After Petrov I met Tanya and at least we had enjoyed our time together no matter what the future might bring. Could it have been more than a coincidence or just luck? I messaged him to see if he was around the next day. I got nothing back.

I feel somewhat ashamed to admit this, but I've been checking on my old friends. Everyone does it from time to time don't they? *I haven't been stalking you or anything, but I noticed that you have a lovely house/dog/spouse.* Are you getting used to it yet? It's a bit like telling someone you had a dream about them. It transgresses the two worlds. There are security settings to lock people out. And why would anyone leave them open if they didn't want to be found? That's how I found Helen again, through a new social media account she'd set up. She hadn't thought to block me. According to the columns of pictures she posted she's having a great life. She's still with her teenage sweetheart. I trawled through the pictures of him, but I don't recognize him at all. He's as far removed from me as it's possible to imagine; muscular, strong in jaw, handsome, perma-tanned and brimming with star quality. If I didn't know better I could have sworn he was one of Helen's famous PR clients; a TV doctor, survival guru or mountaineer. Oh, yes. That's right. He's also a mountaineer. Had she been working on him? She looked happy, a little too made up perhaps and as giddy and excited as a teenage girl. Her updates abounded in excitement. There were surprise trips to Nepal and Thailand, meeting with the parents after so many years apart, friends reunited. I wonder if any of them spared a thought for the castaway? I used to get on really well with them.

I could feel the old me coming back, the sentimental one, and I felt a fondness for my former life that I hadn't felt in quite some time. I began looking up some of my old colleagues. One by one I found most of the creative team from the Wittchety Grub. It wasn't hard, although I did wonder if the contents of what had gone into their profiles might have been vetted by WordFarm. Incredibly, they've only gone and made Max a Creative Director. Max Snodgrass; the home boy, the data geek who thought that everything about an ad had to relate back to the focus groups and the demographics. Oh, well. Even bacteria evolve over time. Natalie has moved on, my old partner in crime, but my old boss and the rest of the team are still there. They're still the essence of our creative team but somehow removed from the reality that I once knew. If they'd kept me on where would I be now?

2nd October

Today I drove to the university to find Petrov through a blinding deluge. The rain rattled down on the surface of the road like the long dotted lines in a children's sketch. By the time I'd pulled in to the car park these thick, heavy raindrops had been replaced by a kind of drizzle and I was able to jog from the car to the entrance to the Department with only a smattering of water soaking into my clothes. I went straight in, taking a sharp turn to the left and up the stairs to his office. The door was open and as I approached I could see the floor littered with boxes full of books and files. Someone was packing.

He turned around and looked at me through an altogether conventional pair of rimless spectacles.

'Can I help you?' he said turning back to filtering through books and throwing them into one of several boxes at his feet.

'Yes, I hope so. I'm here to see Nikola Petrov.'

'Did you have an appointment?'

'Yes.'

'Well I'm afraid you've missed him. He left for the United States.'

'Really? I'm sure he would have told me.'

'Were you expecting to see him before he went?'

'I've got the final draft of an article to discuss with him.'

'Not always the best at keeping everybody informed was our Nikola, especially when he wanted to press ahead with something. And your name is?'

'Richard Kidd.'

'Are you a journalist?'

'No, I'm a freelancer. And a friend'

'Good.' He stopped sifting through the bookshelves and turned around to face me. He was on the young side of middle-aged with a round cherubic face. He didn't smile but slouched into Petrov's seat in his faded jeans and corduroy jacket and looked at me carefully.

'Sorry, I should have said. I'm Matthew Priestley, Professor of Sociology specialising in technology and crime amongst other things. Do you have the article?'

'No.'

'Ok, well I'm sure if you email it to him he'll be able to proof read it.'

He looked at me as if to ask if I might be kind enough to let him resume his packing.

'Thanks. Do you know what he's doing in the States?'

'Yes, he's taken up a post as visiting professor at the Department of Sociology at Stanford. I believe he's going to be working on human-machine relationships. No change there.'

'When's he get back?'

'Oh, he may come back in a year or two. Or not at all. It's up to him.'

'Do you know if he's OK? Did he have any problems when he left?'

'Not that I recall. You know there's the usual stresses and strains of pulling up roots, but Nikola doesn't have a wife or children. He's asked me to send across a few bits and pieces, a few home comforts before he settles in. Did you want me to pass him a message?'

'No that's OK. I'll drop him a line.'

I was too much in shock by this sudden exodus to stick around so I left Priestley to finish packing and locking things up. He might at least have said something or prepared us in some way for his departure. He hadn't even thought to stay around to finish his research or attend to the mess that had erupted over Neil's death. Did he even care about Anna? I thought back to the missed phone calls. It seemed unlikely that he would be so callous but what do I really know about him? Could it be that he had simply taken the opportunity to jump ship at the last minute before things got dangerous?

By the time I had left the building my head was spinning. I had that strange sense of being disconnected from reality once again. I called him. I tried several times but each time it went straight to a voicemail. I headed home and stopped off at the *Wikeekee* café on the way. There was no sign of Vivienne. I took out my tablet and for the first time I began a deep search of his academic profile and credentials, starting with the university website. His picture and profile were still on display but there was no update on his whereabouts. Of course Priestley was right. It was clear from his page that he was only a visiting professor, coming and going as he pleased. His CV included an upbringing in Titoist Yugoslavia and an education at the Faculty of Philosophy at the University of Belgrade. He studied there as an undergraduate from 1981 - 1986. His post-graduate years were spent researching the fields of sociology and medicine as well as the sociology of urban planning. Described in his profile as internationalist in outlook he was active in writing about the break-up of Yugoslavia and was vehemently in favour of its preservation by peaceful means. By 2001 he seemed to have embraced international travel; visiting professor at the Australian National University until 2002, then to the University of Melbourne 2002 -2003, Ohio State University 2003 - 2005, University of Manchester 2005-06, University of Amsterdam 2008 - 09 and now Stanford. I checked his social media profile, his friends and followers. How could I have missed it? Buried beneath the torrent of abusive messages was a farewell message to his UK friends.

Off to sunnier climate and a fresh challenge in the Americas. You can always count on Americans to do the right thing - after they've tried everything else.

Keep in touch with your news and photos. I will be updating my blog when I arrive at the shrine of Sergy and Larry.

The update had received several dozen likes and comments from well-wishers. I trawled through them, this time opening up each of the profiles to find out more about those people who obviously felt the most closely connected to his career, finding not a sea of followers but a host of similar technologists and professors. They were based all over the world; Chile, Mexico, Canada, Australia and of course Silicon Valley. It didn't seem to matter whose profile I clicked on. They were all involved in control groups of every kind. I saw tweets reaching out for volunteers on everything from sexual dysfunction, depression, stress, loneliness, family problems, diet, relationships, inequality at home or at work. Network after network of experimental control groups spreading out across the world and at the head of it all, in the background without being named or mentioned once, I could feel the ever watchful presence of the Capucine programme monitoring their activity. Petrov was part of a collective academic community which may be independent and revolutionary but may equally have fallen into the hands of the venture capitalists. I just couldn't see that far no matter how much I trawled and clicked through the connections he has accumulated. So I went back to the little people, back to us in this city by the sea, Anna, Mark, Steve, Vivienne, Estella, Matilda and Tanya. We were only a small handful of people in a collection of thousands. Did he give a damn about us? I was angry with Petrov and began flicking through his timeline all the way back to before we first met. I scrolled all the way back to the time we first encountered one another. I recognized a photograph. It was the one I took of the World War Two fighter diving into the sea. It had been picked up by one of his journalist friends in the media who had contacted me afterwards. He had

194

circulated some of my photographs of crowds which had been forwarded and broadcast to a wider audience. One of them had been liked by Tanya some time before I met her. I scrolled further and found Steve's account. He'd registered and had begun commenting on everything from planning applications to local fish populations. He was running as a Green candidate in the council elections. Matilda was starting a new job in London. Everything was moving forward. Something was moving us forward too but was this social media account of Petrov's even managed by him? I have my doubts. I felt disorientated and stared out of the windows of the *Wikeekee* to sea, to the world beyond our shores. I couldn't believe that he had just disappeared like that. I had always been a sceptic when it came to his modern adaptation an obscure sociological theory. Is that why he handed me the text? To show me that he was really part of the mainstream? The book he once gave me was a copy of *Walden Two* by the great behaviouralist B.F. Skinner. Was he trying to demonstrate his value as the inheritor of a tradition dating back to post-war social theory, psychoanalysis, nineteenth century utopian socialism, and all the rest stretching back to the dreamers who gazed at the heavens through the first telescopes? I think he was. I think he needed to feel that despite the dangers he was still pursuing something fundamentally noble, expressing humankind's still unfulfilled dream of pursuing the best of all possible worlds.

At the beginning of this journal I said that I was in the business of future prevention. I said I wanted to say farewell to the man inside me before he became consumed by the machine. I addressed this journal to anyone who might be willing to pick it up one day and read it. All along it was probably addressed to someone very much like him. But future prevention is what we long for when we are locked in the darkest corners of our minds. Yet, it's in the nature of our lives that some things are going to happen even if we

195

don't want them to, not least because the scale of our interactions with one another is too vast, too impersonal, too global. What will take place, even the deadening of old emotions and the collapse of our former selves, is not without its advantages if something follows. There is still time. I need to make some changes. The first thing I will do is fulfil a promise to Tanya to exhibit my pictures in the winter festival. I will invite all my new friends as well as the old ones. It will be good to see them again. I will book a weekend flight to Madrid. I will find a way of teaching something. It's useless to hold the tide back. When I look around, I feel as though we are still in danger of becoming a legion of wireless mannequins buffeted by the waves made by others. Perhaps one day there will be a machine that can help restore us to our true potential but until then we are left to act alone. As I left the café and began the walk home, I felt hope in a future that does not need to be prevented. I hope it's still possible to fuse the many parallel strands of this life together into a greater and better version. I hope that one day we will all manage to make a successful escape attempt. May it be the first of many.

Printed in Great Britain
by Amazon

42400819R00112